The Ultimate Truth

Best wishes

Ellen Harduned

The Ultimate Truth

THE POWER OF ONE

Ellen Hardwick

Matador
9 Priory Business Park,
Wistow Road, Kibworth Beauchamp,
Leicestershire. LE8 0RX
Tel: 0116 279 2299
Email: books@troubador.co.uk
Web: www.troubador.co.uk/matador
Twitter: @matadorbooks

ISBN 978 1788037 143

British Library Cataloguing in Publication Data.
A catalogue record for this book is available from the British Library.

Printed and bound by CPI Group (UK) Ltd, Croydon, CR0 4YY
Typeset in 11.5pt Aldine401 BT by Troubador Publishing Ltd, Leicester, UK

Matador is an imprint of Troubador Publishing Ltd

Other books by the Author

Untold Truth
The first book of this trilogy
A spiritual mystery which takes Jane and Mark on a
journey that transforms their lives when they discover
their untold truth.

The Dark Truth – A Crystal Legacy
The second book of this trilogy;
It follows Jane and Mark's journey where Mark's secret
and past is revealed when something happens to the
earth's crystals.

www.ellenhardwick.wordpress.com

CHAPTER ONE

Jane sucked in her breath and grabbed the edge of her car seat as Mark sent the Jeep careering round the bend at reckless speed. The tyres struggled to grip on the loose gravel and it shuddered violently across the road. He braked quickly, spinning the steering wheel back; and as the Jeep straightened, his foot slammed down on the accelerator again.

Jane snatched a look back. The white van had slowed to take the corner, but it wasn't long before it was picking up speed again.

'They're gaining!' she shouted and quickly turned back to the front.

Her mouth went suddenly dry and panic pounded itself into her heart. She needed to remain calm, but the tightening knot in her stomach pulled her focus from the dirt road ahead, allowing fear to attack her mind.

What will happen if they catch us? Will we suffer the same way as Fiona? Why didn't we leave Africa sooner?

She swallowed hard and let her body sink deeper into the seat, resisting any attempt to answer her questions.

Mark glanced in her direction and his face was grim. He didn't say anything and quickly returned to his driving, but in his momentary loss of concentration he had missed seeing the hole gaping across the road. He frantically pulled the wheel round to make the Jeep swerve to miss it.

The momentum pushed Jane's body to the left and then back to the right. She stiffened and gasped in a breath. The rush of speed and the feeling of being out of control was like being in a roller coaster. She had felt like this before, a long time ago, and it had ended badly.

The vehicle straightened again.

She watched Mark's handling of the Jeep. His fast reflexes caught the wheel when it fought to get out of his hands and his sudden braking and fast acceleration avoided most of the holes and low dips in the road that threatened to overturn them.

The Jeep flew over a rise and landed hard, taking Jane completely by surprise. She lifted off her seat, to the roof and back again. The jolt whipped through her back and neck and she cried out in pain.

'Sorry about that!' Mark shouted over the roar of the engine.

Jane rubbed her neck and took another look back. Her eyes widened. The van was so close she could clearly see the men's faces. 'MARK!'

He had already seen them and was hammering the accelerator, cursing under his breath at the lack of speed the Jeep was giving him.

Jane faced the front, her mind screaming, *NO… No more please! I want this to stop!*

Then her phone rang.

Bewildered, she eased it out of her trouser pocket, pressed the answer button and yelled, 'HELLO!'

'Jane, tell Mark to take the second turning on the right.' It was Stan's calm and controlled voice.

'What? How do you know where…?'

'SHUT UP and tell him!'

Jane turned to Mark. 'It's Stan. He says take the second on the right.'

Mark frowned, then nodded.

'Okay,' she confirmed.

'Tell him to follow the road up the mountain. He'll see me in one of the scenic pull offs or what you call lay-bys. Tell him to pull in behind me.'

'Understood.'

The line went dead.

She relayed Stan's instructions and saw Mark nod. The sound of Stan's voice and his clear instructions seemed to settle her fear and worry. She instantly began to feel safe and knew Stan would get them out of this mess.

The first turning came and went like a flash. Mark couldn't risk slowing down; the van was so close.

Jane pushed herself up against the dashboard, concerned they would miss the next one. She strained to see it amongst the dust and rocks of the road.

A glint of light reflected on something. 'There, there,' she yelled, pointing.

'Hang on!' Mark shouted and twisted the wheel to the right while jamming on the brakes. The Jeep skipped sideways and took the turning perfectly. Once they were round, Mark changed gear and was accelerating.

The van overshot and screeched to a stop. It quickly reversed and turned onto the same road. The delay had put more distance between them.

The road went up the side of the mountain. The S-bends were tight and short. Mark swung the Jeep around them as if he had been doing it for years. Behind them, the van kept on coming, but slower, and often going out of sight when they turned each bend.

Jane spotted Stan standing at the side of the road by a lay-by on the outer edge of the mountain. Mark screeched the Jeep to a stop behind him and Jane quickly looked back.

The white van came into view; Stan raised his rifle to his shoulder and fired two shots. Each bullet hit the driver's side front windscreen. The van veered out of control and swung off the road just in front of where Stan was positioned. It seemed to hang in mid-air for a moment before plunging down the mountainside to the bottom of the ravine.

Jane heard a tremendous crash that rumbled through the ground. She got out of the Jeep and ran to where Stan was looking over the edge. He turned and caught her arm, forcing her back.

'You don't want to see it,' he said quietly.

She looked at him, overwhelmed with emotions. Gratitude and relief that he had put a stop to the car chase, but also shock and alarm in that he had just killed two men doing it. She turned away, her stomach heaving.

Mark joined them. He looked as pale as Jane felt. He put his arms around her and said softly, 'Are you all right?'

She nodded, forcing herself to take deep breaths to fight off the sickness, determined not to throw up.

He pulled away and extended his hand to Stan. 'Thanks, mate.'

Stan shook it.

'How did you know where we were?'

Jane saw Stan smile. 'A call from James. He spotted the white van pull out after you when you left. He told me what route you were taking.'

Jane cleared her throat before speaking, but her voice still trembled. 'Did you... have to kill them?'

'Yes,' Stan said abruptly, staring directly at her.

She turned her head away and he gently caught her under the chin, turning her face back to him.

'These people are thugs, Jane. They are not bothered

how badly they hurt you to get what they want. They choose this way of life and the death that comes with it.' He let his hand drop from her face and walked towards the Jeep. 'Great driving, Mark. Give me a hand, will you?'

Jane watched Mark and Stan take the rucksacks from the back of the Jeep and place them on the ground. Stan indicated for Mark to go to the passenger door while he opened the driver's side and released the handbrake. Together they pushed the Jeep over the edge.

Jane's body started to shiver and a wash of coldness touched her skin, despite the heat of the day. She hugged herself. Had they made a mistake staying so long checking the crystals were okay at James' mine? Perhaps if they had left earlier, Ferrand's men wouldn't have caught up with them and not had to die. Part of her felt responsible for their deaths, yet another part wanted to believe they deserved what they got.

Stan beckoned her to follow him. He was headed for a tiny, battered blue car parked at the other end of the lay-by.

'What's this?' Mark scoffed, fingering the rusted door handle. 'Not your usual quality of transport.'

Stan shrugged his shoulders. 'Best I could do at short notice.' He immediately smiled and opened the door for them. 'But just wait until you see our next means of transport.'

CHAPTER TWO

Jane stared at the small, cabinless speedboat gently bouncing against the pontoon. She didn't speak or make any effort to pass Stan the bags. Her body was numb and her legs frozen so she couldn't move. The sounds around her blurred into a mush of tones and indistinguishable words. Sweat seeped from the pores of her skin just below her hairline and yet her skin was cold. She saw in fuzzy vision Mark jump into the boat and extend a hand to her. She didn't move; she couldn't move. She saw him frown and heard him call her name, but her body wasn't registering anything. Its only feeling was a pulse of heat flushing upwards and a rising sickness in her stomach. As the heat wave reached her head it seemed to drain quickly downwards, taking all her blood with it. The last thing she saw was Mark and Stan leaping off the boat and moving towards her.

When Jane opened her eyes she saw Mark's concerned face looking down at her. She was laid on something soft with her head on his lap, cradled in his arms. Behind Mark's head the world swayed from side to side. Her body stiffened as she realised they were on the speedboat she had seen earlier.

Mark held her tightly. 'It's okay, it's okay,' he soothed.

Stan's face appeared above Mark's head and he smiled. 'Glad you're back with us.' He disappeared again.

Jane heard the boat engine start up and felt its rumble along her back. She crunched her body up, bringing her arms across her chest.

Mark frowned and his grip tightened again. 'What's the matter?' he asked.

Jane couldn't speak; the words were stuck in her throat. Instead, she turned fully into him and hid her face in his chest. He held her without speaking and the boat motored out to the open sea.

Jane didn't know how long she stayed huddled into Mark, but it seemed an age before she felt able to lift her head.

Mark kissed her forehead. 'How are you feeling now?'

'Better,' Jane croaked, still snuggled tight against his chest. He offered her a bottle of water and Jane eased one hand away long enough to take the bottle and have a sip. She could feel the small boat thumping through the waves, its engine roaring.

Mark shifted his position.

Jane dropped the bottle and grabbed him. She couldn't control her actions; they were instinctive and automatic.

Stan picked up the bottle and looked at her.

'STAY AT THE WHEEL, STAY AT THE WHEEL!' Jane screamed.

He frowned, gave the bottle to Mark and returned to steering the boat.

An hour later the boat slowed and Jane heard the deep sound of a horn blow once. It sounded high up and very close. She opened her eyes and saw the side of a huge cargo ship rising up on the right side of the speedboat. Stan was manoeuvring the boat under the small, open hatch mid-way up the cargo ship's side where a rope ladder was hanging. He caught the ladder and secured a rope to it.

Jane released her grip from Mark and shot over to the ladder. She caught hold of a rung and hoisted herself up, climbing steadily until she reached the top. Two of the ship's crew helped her over the top rung and onto the deck inside. She took a deep breath as relief spread throughout her body and let herself slide down against the interior wall of the ship, to wait for the others. A few minutes later Mark came through the hatch carrying two rucksacks, but it was a while later before Stan made an appearance.

He threw his rucksack and holdall onto the deck and thanked the ship's crew before turning to her. 'What's going on with you?'

Jane got up slowly and faced him. 'I don't know. I've never reacted like that before.'

Stan didn't have chance to reply for one of the crew interrupted, 'I'll show you to your cabins, it's this way.' He guided them down the corridor towards the stern and at the end he pointed to two doors opposite each other before leaving.

They all went into the cabin on the left. It was small and compact. There were two bunk beds on one side and a chair and round table on the other, next to a door that led to a bathroom. A porthole window allowed them to see out to the sea beyond.

Jane sat down on the bottom bunk and stared at the floor.

'Stan thinks you may be suffering from traumatic shock, as a result of the car chase,' Mark said, sitting down next to her and squeezing her arm.

'It could be what triggered my reaction, I suppose, but...' Jane stopped, remembering the fear of being completely out of control and helpless to do anything. 'I... I had an accident in a small speedboat when I was seventeen...'

Stan sat on the chair and looked at her. 'What happened?'

She sensed they were waiting for an answer, but she wasn't sure she wanted to relive the experience. Finally, she took a deep breath and relayed what happened...

She and her best friend, Amy, were lying on the beach at St Aubin's bay in August, during one of the hottest summers in Jersey. They hadn't been sunbathing for long before Amy raised herself on her right elbow and faced Jane. This was always a sign Amy was bored and wanted to do something.

'Oh no, what is it now?' Jane said, pushing up her sunglasses.

Amy's smile of perfect white teeth was made brighter by her naturally tanned, dark skin. She flicked back a strand of short, black hair and nodded her head towards the shoreline. 'See those boys there.' She pointed to a group of three boys climbing off a speedboat. 'I bet I could get them to take us out on their boat.'

Jane studied the boys. They looked about the same age as her, or maybe a bit older, and all had blondish hair and tanned bodies. 'How much?' she teased.

'An ice cream,' Amy said, getting to her feet.

'Amy, you don't mean to do it, do you?' Jane sat up, feeling a little nervous.

'Yeah, why not?' She brushed her hands down her body, adjusted her cream bikini and strutted down the beach. She approached the boys at the water's edge.

Jane watched with excitement as Amy flirted with them before directing their attention back up the beach to her. She put her hand to her mouth and giggled. *This will be fun if Amy could do it*, she thought. A moment later Amy was waving to her to bring their stuff. Jane picked up their towels and beach bags and made her way down the beach. She felt butterflies in her stomach, but had calmed them by the time she joined Amy at the boat.

Amy introduced her to the boys. 'This is John,' she said, pointing to the boy who was smallest. His short, sandy hair was spiked and when he smiled, his lip curled up to the side.

'This is Mick.' She pointed to the second boy who was shorter than Jane. He had shoulder length, ash-blond hair with a fringe that swept over his eyes. He was more muscular than John and had a deep bronze tan.

'And finally, this is Roy.' The last boy was tall with mousy-coloured hair cut close to his scalp. He had broader shoulders than the other boys, yet the rest of his body was quite thin.

He stepped up to Jane.

'So you fancy coming on the boat?'

Jane nodded nervously and was surprised when he took her hand and guided her to where the boat bobbed up and down on the shoreline. Jane put her bags and towels into the boat and Roy held the boat steady as she climbed in. She quickly found a seat on the far side and waited for Amy to climb in and sit next to her.

When they were settled, Roy expertly jumped in and stood behind the steering wheel, while John and Mick lifted the anchor from the sand, placed it on the bow and pushed the boat out until they were waist-deep in the water. When Roy had lowered and started the engine, John and Mick climbed in and took the seats opposite her and Amy.

The boat gently moved through the water and when they were clear of the beach Roy pushed up the speed. Soon the boat was skipping over the waves to the open sea.

Jane turned to face the front; the wind was pushing into her face and sending her fair hair flying backwards. It felt fantastic, even when her body lifted off the cushion and slammed back again with each wave top they hit.

Amy yelled in excitement and moved off the cushion to stand next to Roy.

Roy spun the wheel, swinging the boat to the right, then to the left, making large circles and figures of eight. Each time he turned, he made the circles tighter.

'Yahoo…' Amy yelled, punching the air with her fist.

Jane laughed at her, but kept her own hand tightly gripped to the boat rail. It was fun, but just a little too wild.

Roy pushed the speed even higher, and with each turn of the wheel the boat curled over, closer to the water. Jane could almost touch the sea on her side, and when the boat swung back again, she found herself hanging on for all she was worth to prevent herself from being thrown to the other side of the boat. She glanced at Amy and saw the scared look on her face.

'I think that's fast enough, Roy!' Amy shouted.

Roy just turned and grinned at her. 'What you say we see what she's got?' he said to no one in particular and pushed the throttle right down. The swing of the boat was frightening. Jane could see Roy was struggling to hold onto the wheel. John and Mick were gripping hard to the railing, their faces reflecting the fear in all of them.

'Roy, please stop!' Amy screamed.

He just laughed at her.

The engine was screaming; Amy was screaming; Jane was too frightened to open her mouth, she just hung on.

The boat hit a wave hard, lifting everyone off their seats. Amy lost her grip on the front seat and went crashing to the floor and into the side lockers. She tried to get a grip of something to pull herself up, but Roy had swung the wheel back round, sending her flying across the bottom of the boat and into Jane's legs. Jane grabbed hold of her.

'For fuck's sake, man, what are you doing?' John shouted at Roy.

Roy glared at him, spun the wheel in the opposite direction and stepped away from it.

The boat screwed tightly round and a large wave caught it on the front edge. It shuddered, before lifting vertically.

Jane tightened her hold on the rail, aware that her body was sliding off the cushions and her feet were losing their grip on the wet floor.

Amy was hanging in mid-air, struggling to hold onto Jane's other hand, her weight dragging at Jane's arm, her nails digging into the flesh of Jane's hand.

There was panic in Amy's eyes as their hands slipped away. She fell, hitting the stern edge hard before catapulting over the side and into the sea.

The boat slammed back down on Jane's side, causing her head to smash into the metal rail. The pain was so intense it nearly made her lose her grip, but she desperately held on with both her hands.

Mick and John lost their grip and crashed into her body before tumbling down towards the front and coming to a stop as their heads impacted against the support poles of the front seats.

Roy was just standing rigid against the back of the driver's seat, his face blank, and his eyes staring past her to the back.

She followed his look at the same time, hearing the screeching of the boat's engine. It rose up out of the water. A black monster of metal, its propeller blades whirling in the air. Jane stared at it in horror, her body fused in position.

The nose of the boat swung upwards, sending the stern of the boat with the engine and its churning blades, back into the sea.

She heard Amy's terrifying scream and the sea suddenly stained red.

Mick and John's unconscious bodies rolled past and bounced over the stern.

She turned to look at Roy. His eyes were wide and his mouth was open in a silent scream as he clung to the front seat.

Jane let go of the rail and pushed off the side lockers with her feet. She felt the force of the boat lift her, and then nothing but air until she hit the sea.

Moments later she surfaced, gasping for air. The boat lay upside down not far from her, the engine silent and the propeller still. She could see no one else…

★ ★ ★

'They all died,' Jane said, her voice breaking. 'My best friend…' She stopped speaking, tears filling her eyes.

Mark put his arm around her. 'I'm so sorry,' he said gently.

Jane wiped away the tears. 'I know it was a long time ago, but after that I just couldn't go on a speedboat again.'

Stan nodded and stood up. 'It's not surprising you reacted as you did. The ordeal you experienced in the Jeep must have triggered the emotions linked to this event, sending your body into shock. You did okay, though. Now both of you rest and I'll see you later.' He left the cabin.

Jane got up and fetched some water from her rucksack. She gave some to Mark who, after drinking, stretched out onto the bottom bunk. He looked exhausted.

'Why don't we have a sleep?' he said, moving over and patting the bed beside him. 'Let's rest together.'

★ ★ ★

Several hours later Jane woke up. Mark was still asleep, but she was restless. The memory of Amy was still on her mind, and she needed some fresh air. Quietly, she left the cabin and followed the narrow passageway to the left towards the stern of the ship. A bulkhead door opened on to a small deck area overlooking rows and rows of containers.

She rested her arms on the guard rail and breathed in deeply. The air felt cool and fresh.

The cargo boat's stern was huge and she could just see the wash from the ship's propellers. Her loss of control worried her. She had been unable to function, paralysed by fear that she hadn't realised was from the events of the past.

She sensed a presence behind her and turned to see Stan standing against the outer door watching her. He came over to the rail.

'How are you?' he asked softly.

Jane smiled. 'Better, I just don't know what happened.'

'You've been through some scary stuff, and combined with what you experienced in that boat, your body just shut down.'

'I thought I was stronger than that,' she moaned.

'You will be now.'

Stan's phone beeped and he looked at the message displayed. He chuckled.

Jane was curious. 'What is it?'

He shook his head, smiling. 'It's just Fiona.'

'Is she all right?'

Stan nodded and grinned. 'She's good, really good.'

Jane looked at him, puzzled.

'Yes, Fiona is well and recovering. She's also one hell of a woman.'

Jane laughed, 'I know what you mean. She's got to you then?'

'In more ways than you can imagine.'

Jane saw a glint in his eyes and softness in his face before he turned to face the rail.

'How do you do these things?' she asked.

'What things?' He didn't look at her.

'Getting us out of Africa on a ship like this?'

He raised his left hand and rubbed his forefinger and thumb together.

'It can't just be money?'

He turned right around so his back was to the rail. 'I have friends.'

Jane focused on him. 'And why are you helping us? We haven't paid you or given you anything.'

She saw Stan hesitate as if thinking about what he should say. 'It's a favour for James,' he finally said and then changed the subject. 'I think it is time for something to eat. Let's get Mark.' He walked to the open door and paused to wait for her.

Jane was puzzled by his reaction. Something wasn't right, but what it was, she didn't know.

CHAPTER THREE

James got into his battered, rusty, old Mercedes and drove through the open gates of his house in Namibia. He had received a text from Stan confirming Mark and Jane were safe and he felt good. Nestled in the inside pocket of his cotton jacket was his Lola, the morphed master crystal in the shape of a heart. He could feel Lola's energy and love radiating into his body as if she was touching him with her hand. She often came to him in his dreams and many times he hadn't wanted to wake up, but he knew life must go on and he was so lucky to have her essence with him every day.

The journey to his mine didn't take long and the security man waved him through as usual. His office shack was deep into the open-cast mine and he drove down the rough track to it. Business had taken off since Mark and Lola had cured the crystals and he liked to think it was due to the fact that Lola's love and compassion were vibrating in every crystal his mine uncovered. He opened the office door, switched on his computer and settled down to the day's work.

Two hours later, he heard a car draw up outside. He was curious as to how the car had got so far into the mine without him being notified. He could only assume it was government officials come to inspect the mine. They often turned up unexpectedly and his security officer would have allowed them in. He got up from his chair and went to the door.

The door burst open and two white, unshaved men, dressed in khaki trousers and shirts, blocked his way. James knew from their stance they were not officials, but most likely mercenaries. He stepped back as they moved into the room.

'And what can I do for you, gentlemen?'

The taller of the two, his face chubbier than a baby's, his eyes narrower than the gaps between paving stones, smiled and ran a grubby hand through the straw-like hair dishevelled around his head. 'Information. We are after some information.'

James backed into the front edge of the desk and paused. 'Yes, of course. Please take a seat.' He glanced past the tall guy and his smaller companion to the car outside where two more white men were leaning against the bonnet, smoking. Cautiously, he slid along the side of the desk to his seat and sat down. 'What is it you need to know?'

The tall man sat down and crossed one leg over the other. He looked relaxed and obviously confident he was in control. 'Your friends, where are they?'

James looked at him, puzzled. 'Friends? What friends are you referring to?'

The man pounced on him and drove a flick knife into the shoulder joint of his right arm. James yelled and tried to pull back, but the man grabbed the back of his neck and forced his head down onto the desk before applying more pressure to the wound.

James clenched his teeth.

'Where have your friends gone?'

'I... I don't know,' he spluttered.

More weight came down onto James' head. His vision blurred and his head spun with the crushing force of the man's hands. 'I don't know! I don't know!' he screamed.

The pressure eased and the tall man transferred a hand to

his neck, pinning him down while searching his jacket side pockets. He found James' phone.

'Your code to open it,' he demanded.

James shook his head.

The man slammed the knife into his right shoulder again. '4551, 4551,' James cried out.

The man entered the numbers and opened the message app.

James watched him read Stan's last message. Fortunately, Stan had only said they were getting on a cargo ship and not where they were going.

The man released James and moved back into the room. He pulled out his own phone from his trouser pocket and dialled a number. 'A cargo ship, sir. No indication where it was going. Yes, should be easy enough to trace where they got on it, given their last location.' He lowered his voice and said something else.

James knew he was asking the other person what he should do with him. It wasn't hard to guess what the answer was going to be. James eased his left hand down to the desk drawer and quietly slid it open. His fingers curled round the grip of his loaded revolver and he drew it up under him in readiness. A slight breeze brushed the back of his neck and he knew the window behind him was open.

The tall man put his phone back and nodded to his companion as he made for the door.

The companion grinned and went for the gun concealed in the back of his trouser waistband.

James leapt up, his gun firing twice, the bullets hitting the smaller man in the chest. He caught a glimpse of the tall man turning back into the room as he twisted to his right and threw himself through the window. The landing was a bit rough, but he was soon on his feet and running down the track into the mine.

A car started up and he heard the scream of its engine as it sped down the road after him. It would soon be upon him and James knew his only chance was to go into the blast area. Here at least he could get into areas the car couldn't go. He swerved off the track and through an opening to a large area where mounds of rock littered the floor. As he passed the largest one, he heard gunshots behind him and saw stone splinters ricochet off the rocks close to him.

A siren sounded several times and James knew he was in trouble. The blasting was still going on and he was headed straight into it. He had no choice; either way, he was facing death. The first blast rocked him off his feet, catapulting him several yards to the right. The second blast threw him back and showered him with piles of rock. And when the third blast came, the whole world seemed to crash down upon him and darkness engulfed him.

James came to consciousness with the pain and the knowledge he was still alive. Flecks of light penetrated the darkness around him and he was able to see that he had fallen between two large rocks that had prevented an even larger piece of rock from crushing him. It had instead sealed him in a rocky tomb.

He tried to move his legs, but the pain made it impossible for him to ease them more than an inch. He guessed one or more bones were broken. A warm feeling of love and compassion centred on his heart and he reached into his jacket pocket and pulled out his crystal. He could feel Lola and knew she was with him.

The streams of light coming in through the joints between the rock meant that it was still daylight and he wondered how long had passed since the incident. Outside there was no sound and he kept silent, waiting to hear if anyone was still after him. Time went by and still he quietly waited.

After a while, a garbled sound started to come from a distance and as it got closer he was able to distinguish that it was voices, many voices: African voices. It gave him hope and he kissed Lola before putting the crystal back into his pocket.

It was time. 'HELP! HELP!'

Minutes later, James heard a familiar sound: people speaking a language that used clicking sounds. The scraping of metal against rock came next and soon the joint between the large rock above him and the ones either side widened, letting in more light. More chattering of the language and many hands came either side of the rock and it began to move, creating an opening big enough for him to get through. He smiled when a familiar face came into view. 'Fred, I'm so glad to see you.'

Fred smiled back. His rich, copper skin shining in the sun's rays and his black peppercorn hair partly covered by a hat. He reached down to James, grabbed him under the armpits and pulled him through the opening.

James ignored the pain that came with the crunching sound of the bones in his legs as they ground together and instead focused on the many hands now supporting and carrying him back through the mine. At the shack they laid him on the floor and Fred treated his wounds with herbs and plant medicine before binding his legs together with wood and material.

'Ambulance is coming,' Fred said, wiping the sweat from James' face. 'It will take time for them to come, so I have treated you.'

James nodded in thanks. Already, the pain was easing with

whatever Fred had placed on his legs. 'What happened to the men who were after me?'

Fred spoke to one of the other men in the room, before he said, 'Dead, except one who drove away.'

James grabbed his friend's hand. 'I've got to warn Stan, I need a phone.'

Fred took the cloth bag off his bare back and searched inside. He grinned at James as he handed him a mobile phone.

James stared at it. 'I see you've upgraded to the top model.' The image of his bushman friend, out in the desert, using a smartphone, never did seem right to him.

'It also does banking,' Fred chuckled.

James laughed and within minutes he was talking to Stan.

CHAPTER FOUR

Jane had just finished eating a cooked meal of beef stew and dumplings followed by fruit and jelly when Stan's phone rang. He answered it and his face paled.

'How bad is it?' There was a muffled reply.

'Don't worry about us. Tell Fred to get you out of the hospital to a safe place once they set your legs.'

Jane looked across at Mark and saw the concern on his face too.

'Text me when you're safe.' Stan rang off and relayed to them what James had told him.

Jane didn't know what to say or do. She felt sick at the thought of James nearly dying.

Mark thumped the table, making them all jump. 'This can't keep happening,' he fumed. 'It has to stop!'

Stan placed a hand on his shoulder. 'It will.'

Mark pushed his chair back and stood up. 'I… I need some fresh air.' He left the room.

Jane watched him go, her heart sinking at his hurt. He must be worried about his own family too. She turned back to Stan. 'Is there anything we can do for James?'

'No. They think he is dead, which is good.'

'Poor James. Oh, Stan, what are we going to do?'

Stan moved across to sit beside her. 'We do what we said we would do. James will be okay now; he's a tough nut.'

Jane could not picture James being a tough nut, an eccentric one, maybe. She smiled inwardly, remembering their time together in Africa and her conversation with him when they were in the desert. He never did tell her how he had met Stan. 'So how did you two meet?'

Stan poured two cups of coffee and handed her one. 'James saved my life when a contract I was doing went wrong.'

He was waiting for a reaction from her, but when she didn't respond, he just smiled and began telling her his story…

★ ★ ★

Stan picked up the ringing phone, recognising the number on the digital display as his contact Smiley. It was a nickname Stan had given him because nothing seemed to stop the man from smiling. When things went wrong, he smiled; when things went right, he smiled; and when things were disastrous, he smiled.

'Yes,' Stan answered.

'I have a job… if you want it,' Smiley said, a slight hesitation in his voice. 'It's a contract killing. No questions, just a name and place.'

'You know I don't do that.'

'I know, I know, but I don't have anyone else. Call it a favour to me.'

For a moment Stan had a vision of a non-smiling Smiley, so he said, 'Are you in trouble?'

'No, no,' Smiley said, a little too quickly. 'Please, Stan, I need this.'

Stan heard him swallow, before he said, '150 grand, one shot, easy target.'

Stan didn't reply. Contract killings were quick money, but when he chose to do one, he usually only did the ones he felt deserved it. This was an unknown one and he didn't like it. The silence must have worried Smiley.

'200 grand, Stan. Please, mate; I'm desperate.'

'Okay, give me the details. I'll call you to confirm it's a go when I'm ready.' Stan heard Smiley sigh. 'But this is it, Smiley; don't ask again.'

Stan wrote down the details of the place and the name of the target, then put down the phone. *Damn it, Smiley, this is your last favour*, Stan thought and got his high powered scope and M86 sniper rifle from the cupboard.

★ ★ ★

It took him several days to scope the place and identify the target. The man was living in Johannesburg, South Africa, in a modest, well-protected hotel. The building opposite it was a chapel with a tall bell tower on a flat roof with turrets: an ideal place to shoot from. The day before the job, Stan called Smiley.

'Is it still a go?' he asked stiffly.

'Yes, yes.' Smiley's voice seemed a pitch higher than normal. 'When are you doing it?'

'Tomorrow, early.'

'Good, okay...' Smiley cleared his throat, then quickly said, 'Watch your back.' He rang off.

Stan looked at the phone, not sure what to read into that. Smiley never wished him luck or told him to be careful. Something didn't feel right. He dialled Smiley back, but the phone just rang continuously. He switched it off and thought, *A simple job, one shot, an easy target, is what Smiley said. Maybe it isn't going to be that easy.*

24

He got to the chapel before dawn and parked his vehicle in the small street by the chapel's back door. He felt relaxed knowing the preparations had gone smoothly and his escape route was planned. Quietly, he got out of the car, slipping the keys into his shirt pocket and leaving it unlocked. From the boot he pulled out a long, black bag and swiftly walked to the chapel's back door. It was old and the lock rusty, making it easy for Stan to force it open. He stooped and picked up two pebbles from the street, wedging one between the door and its surround, making sure his exit could not be hindered.

The wooden stairs up to the roof creaked and groaned with each step, the sound echoing into the empty building. At the top, he eased the lockless door open and jammed the second pebble under it to prevent it from closing. More stairs went up to the bell tower, but Stan moved out onto the gravel roof. He went to the edge facing the hotel and put his bag down at the place where he was going to take the shot. Carefully, he checked the area around him, before unzipping the bag and putting his sniper rifle together. Once it was done, he got himself into position between the roof turrets.

The target was always punctual, leaving the hotel at 8.15 just as the sun was rising. Stan could see the sky was brightening and he nestled the rifle butt softly into his shoulder. He checked his watch, it was 8am. A quarter of an hour to go.

Through the scope he could see into the hotel's windows. Some had the curtains drawn, while others were open and he could see the occupants moving around inside. The hotel roof was empty except for the birds, and below in the street a few people were moving around while the odd car started up and drove off. Stan turned his gaze back to the hotel door, focusing his attention on the position of the cross hairs.

There was a crunch of a footfall on the roof gravel behind him.

He swung round, bringing the rifle with him.

Three men were at different distances from his position and he shot the one closest in the chest.

The two other men sprinted towards him, their weapons firing.

Bullets sprayed the stony ground where he lay, and he flung himself into a roll to reach the place where the body of the first man had fallen. A bullet caught him in the right shoulder, making him drop his rifle and forcing him away from the body that was shielding him. He snatched the handgun from the dead man's hand and fired two more shots.

The second closest man dropped to the floor.

The third man was now upon him.

Stan took two more bullets before empting his own gun completely into the man's body.

The man fell onto him.

Stan knew his situation was bad; the whole of his right side was screaming in agony and he had to use his left arm to shove the body off him. He took a deep breath and pushed himself up to a sitting position to survey the damage. A bullet had sliced a hole through his right side and another had ploughed into his right thigh, which was bleeding badly.

He crawled across the roof to where his rifle lay, leaving a streak of blood behind him. The gunfire would have attracted attention and if there were any more men waiting in the chapel he needed to be armed. He grabbed the rifle, aimed it at the doorway and waited. Seconds ticked by and no one came.

Stan lowered the rifle and tore off a piece of his shirt to wrap round his bleeding thigh. Then he took the butt end of his rifle and placed it under his armpit to use like a crutch so he could get to his feet. Once he was up, he realised his right leg would not support him, so he slung the rifle across his body and hopped to the roof door, retrieving the second dead man's gun from the floor. The door was still wedged open and no one was about.

He listened as he approached the stairs for any evidence more men were waiting for him down below. There was only silence. He hopped onto the first two steps and lost his footing, sending him tumbling and rolling down the remaining stairs. The handgun flew from his hand as he crashed onto the rock slabs at the bottom.

He lay for a moment catching his breath, hoping he was alone, for if he wasn't, he was going to be dead in the next few seconds. Those seconds passed without incident. He pushed himself up, grabbed hold of the banister and got to his feet. His vision blurred and he became light-headed. One of the bullets must have caught a vein or artery and it was making him weaker with every movement he made. He needed to get help quickly.

The back door was wide open and he fell into a heap on the road beside his car. The keys were still in his shirt pocket and he fished them out with his left hand, but when he reached up to open the door, his strength had left him and his hand slipped from the handle.

At that moment, someone turned him onto his back. A pale face with long, curly hair came into view. There was a gasp of shock.

Stan held up the car keys and shouted, 'If you value your life, get me out of here, quickly.'

The man took the keys and helped Stan into the back of

the car. When he got into the front seat, Stan heard him say in a croaky voice, 'You need to get to a hospital.'

'NO!' Stan yelled, and when the terrified man looked at him he pointed a bloody finger to the dashboard and a piece of paper in the cigarette ash tray. 'Take me there.'

The man took the paper, read the address, then started the car and pulled away…

★ ★ ★

Jane couldn't take her eyes from Stan's emotionless face. She knew hers had gone pale. Stan smiled at her. 'And that's how I met James.'

'Bloody hell!' Jane turned back to the table and fingered her coffee cup.

'James saved my life and so when he needs a favour I help him out.'

So many questions were in her head. 'Who were the men?'

'That's what I wanted to know, so when I had recovered, I went to see Smiley.'

Jane looked at him. 'He betrayed you?'

'No, he was dead and so was his family.'

Jane's eyes widened.

'Smiley had been desperate all right. I think they killed him after my call.'

'Why?'

'Money, maybe. I don't know. The client he was dealing with didn't pay up and I think sent those men to clean up.'

'And the man you were sent to kill?' Jane held her breath.

'I didn't kill him. He was lucky, I guess, because he's still alive.'

'So what was it all for?'

'Beats me, but Smiley left me a clue as to who the client was.'

'And you're going to kill him?' Jane was horrified.

'Yes, when I find him. He's clever though. He's rarely out in public and changes address frequently. But I am biding my time.'

Jane shivered. Death surrounded Stan and it worried her. Yet somehow she always felt safe with him. Safe because he was on their side; and safe, because despite what she was hearing about his life, she felt he was a man of moral principles.

Stan must have been sensing what she was thinking. 'You don't need to worry, Jane; I won't bring any harm to you.'

She took a deep breath. 'Thank you, and thank you for being here with us and for being there for Fiona. Without you…' Jane suddenly felt emotional and stood up, looking away.

Stan got up, turned her back to face him and pulled her into his arms. Jane didn't resist, it felt so good to feel his strength. There had been a strong connection with him in Africa and she began to feel that same desire for him again. It felt deep and old, but not love in the way she loved Mark. When she looked up he was close, bearing down on her. It would be so easy to let it happen, but she pulled away.

He put his arm around her shoulders and gave her a squeeze. 'You should go to Mark. He needs you. He needs reassuring that what he is doing is right,' he said.

Jane nodded. For some reason her whole body felt drained with a deep exhaustion that even sleep would not refresh. Stan walked her to the cabin. She looked at him as she opened the door. 'Thank you, for everything.'

He just smiled and walked away.

CHAPTER FIVE

It was early morning and Jane was packing the last few things in her rucksack. She was sad to be leaving. It had been sixteen days since they had arrived on the cargo ship and Jane had enjoyed every minute of the normality. It had allowed her to rest, busy herself with washing her clothes and also learn about the ship and the techniques used in sailing her. The captain had been quite charming.

Jane missed having a normal life.

Mark, on the other hand, had spent most of the trip worrying about the time it was taking. He was desperate to ensure his family was safe. Stan's original plan was to have them off the grid so Ferrand wouldn't know where they were, but since they had received James' call, Mark had convinced himself Ferrand would find them.

Jane trusted Stan and he seemed unconcerned that Ferrand knew they were on a cargo boat. He pointed out that quite a few ships had left Africa at the same time and Ferrand would not know which one they had intercepted.

The packing took minutes due to the mimimal clothes she had with her and what she did have was not going to be suitable for the cold winter weather England was experiencing. Her thin walking trousers wouldn't protect her from the chill of the wind and the only thing keeping her warm at the moment was a dark blue jumper one of the crew had given her.

Mark zipped up his rucksack and glanced across to her. 'You feeling all right?'

Jane nodded and closed her rucksack. Part of her was anxious about what was to come, yet she knew she couldn't leave Mark to do it alone. Something was urging her to stay close to him.

He came over and rubbed his hand down her back. 'I'll be right beside you, don't worry,' he said.

Jane frowned and then realised he was talking about their departure from the ship. He was obviously concerned she was feeling nervous about it.

She smiled back at him. 'I'll be fine.' But now she was wondering if she would be. 'Let's get some breakfast,' she said hastily.

She opened the cabin door and almost bumped into Stan who was emerging from the cabin opposite. He looked worried and had binoculars in his hand.

'What's the matter?

Stan raced down the corridor to the stern without answering her.

She followed with Mark close behind.

Stan exited onto the deck area and scanned the horizon with the binoculars.

'What is it?' Jane asked again.

'We have company. A small trawler has been trailing us overnight. It's still there this morning.'

'Perhaps it's fishing.'

Stan looked at her. 'Do you see them fishing?' He gave her the binoculars.

Jane felt a little uncomfortable, but looked through them. It was a few minutes before she located the boat. Stan was right, there was no fishing equipment in the water. 'They could be on their way back to port, couldn't they?'

Stan took the binoculars from her and scanned the boat

again. 'No, I don't think so. The boat is quite high out of the water, which means they are not carrying any weight.' He lowered the binoculars. 'I wish I had a bazooka with me.'

'Now that would be something,' Mark chirped in.

Jane stepped back, not believing what she was hearing. 'They could be innocent fishermen and your first thought is to blow them out of the water. There must be another way.'

'Are there no rules about where they can fish?' Mark asked.

Stan smiled. 'There are. I'm going to see the captain. Are you both ready to leave?'

'Yes. But what are you going to do?' Jane asked nervously.

'I'm going to report them to the Fisheries Protection Agency. It might just give us enough time to get off the ship without them knowing.'

After breakfast, Jane and Mark were in their cabin when they heard the ship's horn and felt a slight shudder as the boat started to slow down to steerage speed. There was a knock on the cabin door and it opened. Stan's smiling face peered in.

'Time to go,' he said spritely.

'And the trawler?' Mark asked.

'The plan worked. The fisheries protection vessel has intercepted them and we are some distance away now. Our captain has also moved the ship into a position where we won't be seen leaving it, should anyone be looking.'

'That's good news and... no one gets hurts,' Jane said, prodding a finger onto Stan's chest. He ignored her and moved down the corridor to where two crewmen were preparing to open the exterior bulkhead door, the same one they had entered through when they came onto the ship. The ship's horn blew again and the door was opened and a rope ladder secured to the floor.

Jane was noticing her emotions, wondering whether she was able to control them this time. She did feel different, there was no fear.

Stan faced her. 'The boat isn't a small one, so it'll be okay.' He tied a strap around her waist just under the life jacket the crew had given her and attached it to himself.

She was wondering why he was doing it when he said, 'I'll step out first and you come when I beckon you. We'll go together, right?'

She nodded.

Stan lowered himself a few rungs and Jane turned to face the ship's side as she got onto the first rung. Stan moved into her back and she heard his voice at her ear.

'One rung at a time, slow and steady. Don't look down.'

They moved as one until Stan reached the last rung, a foot away from the boat below. 'Wait here,' he said, adjusting the strap between them so it was longer, before expertly leaping into the stern of the boat alongside the ship.

Jane looked down; the boat was a medium-sized luxury boat with a large open back and a flybridge so steering could be done either inside or up top. She didn't feel any emotional turmoil like previously; in fact, she felt incredibly calm.

Stan pulled the strap between them taut.

She twisted round so half of her body was facing him, took his offered hand and stepped onto the side of the boat as it lifted towards her on the waves. The effortless transfer surprised her and him.

Once she was in the stern, he removed the strap between them before helping her to the seat next to the steering wheel, where the boat's captain was controlling the boat. Then he went back to help Mark.

Jane felt really pleased with herself and relaxed in the

seat, letting her attention focus on the captain. He was a bearded man about fifty years old, with grey, receding hair. His red sailor's jacket and waterproof trousers made him look bigger than he was. He didn't seem to notice her at all. His concentration was focused on continually adjusting the throttle and steering wheel in response to the waves' effect on the boat, keeping it close to, but not touching the cargo ship.

When Mark was on board, Stan reached up and detached the rope holding their luggage. He gave a wave to the ship's crew.

'All clear, Frank,' he called to the captain, who immediately turned the wheel and headed away from the cargo ship at slow speed. Stan went along the side of the boat to the front and pulled up the several buoys that had helped keep the boat from clashing against the cargo ship's side. As soon as Stan was back in the cockpit, the captain pushed the throttle forward and the boat gained speed, cruising through the waves.

Stan slapped him on the back. 'Great to see you, Frank.'

'It's been a while, Stan.' Frank glanced towards Jane and Mark.

Stan introduced them. 'This is Jane and Mark.'

'Pleased to meet ya,' he murmured, returning his view to where the boat was going.

Stan opened the glass cabin door to the inside and indicated for Mark and Jane to go in. The interior was luxurious. To the right, the seats formed a U shape and were made of thick, soft, white leather. The table, cupboards and wood surrounds were highly polished. On the left was a small kitchen area with all the necessary equipment, and further into the boat, down some steps, was the sleeping area and toilet.

Jane slipped onto the leather seat next to Mark and

snuggled into him. She could feel his body was tense. 'Are you still worried about your family?'

'Yes. I keep thinking about what happened to James and Fiona. They could have both been killed and it's my fault.'

'But you weren't to know this would happen.' Jane squeezed his hand.

'If I had given Ferrand what he wanted right at the beginning, things wouldn't have got like this.'

'No, they would have been worse. You said it yourself in Africa.'

Mark's body slumped into the leather. 'I just don't want anyone else to get hurt,' he sighed.

She rested her head on his shoulder. 'Things will be okay, you'll see.'

Her words were positive, but the feelings in her body were telling her something else. She ignored them and closed her eyes, imagining what her life would be like without Ferrand.

She didn't know she had drifted off to sleep until a sudden movement from Mark woke her.

'Sorry,' he said. 'Didn't mean to wake you so abruptly, but we are close to land.'

Jane moved to the window and saw the coastline getting closer. 'How long has it been, and where are we?'

'A couple of hours, I think; and this is the south of England, Cornwall maybe?'

She saw Stan's legs go past the window towards the front. The boat was now entering a small harbour nestled into a cove. It slowed as it approached a row of floating bouys. Stan hauled in some lines attached to one of them and fastened a rope to the cleat at the front. The engine stopped.

Jane and Mark emerged from the cabin. The sun was obsured by low cloud and it felt really cold.

Frank turned to them. 'You'll go ashore in the dinghy with Stan. It'll take four people, so plenty big enough for you all. I have a small two-bedroomed holiday flat overlooking the harbour that you can use.'

'Thank you, Frank,' Jane said. 'I …'

He held up his hand. 'I don't need to know your business. I just ask you to leave the place as you find it.'

Jane nodded.

Stan pulled the dinghy to the side. 'Once you're in the flat, Frank and I are going to take the boat round to its winter mooring. I'll come back in Frank's car. It'll be late, so expect me.'

Jane followed Stan into the dinghy, conscious he was watching her for any signs she would flip, but she felt okay and settled herself at the front on a small bench seat. She stared over the side into the dark blue water and dipped her fingers into it. It was icy cold and she quickly pulled them back out.

Frank cast them off and Stan rowed them ashore to a wooden ladder on the harbour wall. He secured the dinghy to it and they climbed the ladder. It was a short walk along the harbour pier before they turned onto the main street, which followed the beach around the cove.

Jane glanced at the small cottage houses lining one side of the promenade and then across to the beach that was on the other side. This was winter and everything looked grey, damp and bleak, but she could imagine how it would be transformed when summer came and the sun was out.

A brisk wind from the north sent daggers of coldness through her jumper and she folded her arms across her chest to hold in the warmth.

They turned up a side street and stopped at a light blue door.

Stan opened it and gave Mark the key. 'Don't go out and don't contact anyone. There's food in the fridge.'

'When are you back?' Mark asked.

Stan shrugged his shoulders. 'Could be around midnight, maybe later.' He glanced towards the harbour. 'I have a friend to catch up with.' He looked back. 'You have the only key. I'll call Jane's mobile when I'm back, but I'll also knock three times. Check the viewer to make sure it's me before you open up.' He looked up and down the empty street, then left.

Jane stepped into the square hallway that immediately led to some stairs. She was relieved to be out of the cold weather. Her teeth were clenched and her body was shivering as she climbed the stairs to the upper floor.

Mark closed and locked the door.

As she reached the top, she took a moment to absorb the warmth coming from the radiator on the landing, and when Mark joined her, she took her rucksack and moved along the narrow corridor that had five open doors leading from it.

The first room opposite the top of the stairs was a small double bedroom with windows overlooking the street and front door. The second room was a kitchen with all the essentials: sink, cooker, small fridge and washing machine. The third room was a small compact bathroom with shower-bath, sink and toilet. The last two rooms were at the end of the corridor and led to the lounge area and a double bedroom that had large windows overlooking the bay and harbour.

Jane walked into the lounge and dumped her rucksack on the sofa. The place was cosy and warm but her body would not stop shivering. She hugged herself while she looked out of the window and watched Stan return to the boat.

Mark came up behind her, slipping his arms around her waist. 'You're cold, why don't you go for a shower?'

She turned into him, snuggling into his warm body. 'This feels much better.'

He laughed and kissed the top of her head.

For a moment it felt like they were on holiday, then her mind brought reality back. 'I can't believe we are doing this. It feels like we are living in another world, doesn't it?'

Mark just hugged her tighter.

She looked up into his face. 'I'm glad Stan is with us. If anyone is a match for Ferrand, he is.' She saw him frown. 'What is it?'

'Ferrand's a dangerous man and he has a lot of resources available to him. I hadn't realised how dangerous he was until he got to my mother. I know he won't stop until he has got what he wants from me.' He paused and kissed her forehead. 'But perhaps Stan won't stop either.'

'Do you think he enjoys doing this?'

'Who, Ferrand?'

'No. Stan, of course.' But it made Jane think that maybe Ferrand also enjoyed what he did.

Mark shrugged his shoulders. 'I expect he does. It looks like he was in the military and it must be hard for men like him to go back to normal living when they've been trained to kill.'

'Yes, normal living,' she sighed, pulling away from Mark's arms. 'That seems a long time ago.'

It wouldn't be hard for her to return to it when all of this was finished. But how would it end? How could it end? How was Mark going to stop Ferrand? Would they survive what was to come?

She picked up one of the paperback books strewn on the coffee table and flicked through the pages, not seeing any of the words. When she came to the end she put it back and moved to the small cupboard under the TV and scanned the titles of the DVDs.

'We'll have to amuse ourselves for the rest of the day,' Mark said as he relaxed on the sofa.

Jane looked at him sideways and saw him beam a smile in her direction.

'We've plenty to watch and read,' she said, pointing to the books and DVDs. She saw him throw back his head and moan before she added, 'And plenty of time for that.'

His smile broadened and he patted the sofa next to him. She joined him and snuggled against his chest. 'So you think your parents are in England?'

'Yes,' Mark said, confidently.

'Why?'

'Because the only place I can think they would be isn't known to anyone apart from me and them.'

'How can you be so sure they are there?' Jane fingered the top button of his shirt.

'I asked Stan to use his resources to locate them and the only thing he could come up with was a plane ticket from Phoenix to Heathrow, then nothing.'

'So where do we go from here?' Jane was intrigued.

Mark pondered for a moment. 'Not sure if I should tell you,' he teased.

Jane pushed him away and folded her arms across her chest with a big huff.

He laughed and pulled her into him, kissing the side of her face before moving down to her earlobe. He whispered, 'Yorkshire. We'll need a car, and it looks like Stan has that covered too.'

CHAPTER SIX

The next morning they were up early. Stan had returned just after midnight and was now drinking coffee in the kitchen. He smiled when they joined him.

'Did you enjoy your time with Frank?' Jane asked.

'Yes, it's been a few years since I last saw him.'

Jane didn't ask him anything else; she knew he wouldn't have told her anyway. Stan's past was perhaps better left in the past. Instead, she cooked up a breakfast of bacon, egg and sausage.

Everything was cleaned up and made tidy within an hour and they left the flat just as the sun was rising in the sky. Frank's car was a modern silver Ford Fiesta. The seats were comfortable with plenty of leg room and luggage space, although the only luggage they had was their rucksacks and Stan's black holdall.

Stan handed them each a coat from the boot. 'A present from Frank,' he said and got into the driver's seat. 'Where to, Mark?'

'Keighley, West Yorkshire,' Mark replied, then added, 'I'll give you more directions when we're there.'

Stan nodded and they headed north using the M5 and M6 to get to the M62. They made good time, reaching the Halifax turn-off in four hours. From Halifax to Keighley the progress was slower as they were driving through little villages.

Jane saw terraced houses lining the road with black, soot-covered brick walls and occasionally, huge empty buildings of old industrial mills, with their tall chimneys and broken or boarded-up windows. She guessed the drab and dirty-looking houses were the result of the stuff the mills' chimneys used to pour out.

The road continued out of the small villages into moorland, where more modern buildings and pubs were sparsely set between the miles of fields and moors. The cloudy sky dampened the colour of the land, making it look cold and dreary.

They entered the district of Crossroads, on the outer reaches of Keighley, and Mark guided Stan to a narrow road, which took them to the valley floor and under a bridge. The car climbed up the other side of the valley and at the top they turned left onto a road to an isolated village at the very top of the moors. The views were spectacular.

Very few houses made up the village, which consisted of a small lane running along the moor hillside. Stan followed the lane until they came upon a set of terraced houses. Mark got Stan to stop in front of the second to last house.

Jane looked out from the back seat. There was nothing spectacular about the house. It was a two-level terraced home made of Yorkshire stone, with a door and three windows facing the road. A little porch ran along its entire front, protecting the entrance from the weather.

Mark looked at her and Stan. 'I'll see if they're here,' he said quietly.

Stan nodded and left the car running.

Jane felt a flush of nervousness. She hadn't really prepared herself to see Mark's family. What would they be like? Would they like her?

Mark got out of the car and gently closed the door. He walked up the three steps to the open porch and knocked on the door. His hands moved behind him as he waited, his fingers interlocking and twisting round each other.

Jane saw the net curtain, in the window by the door, move and a moment later the door opened about two inches, restricted by the visible chain inside.

Mark leaned in slightly and said something she couldn't hear. There was a moment of hesitation as if the person behind the door was thinking about something. Maybe they were trying to recognise who was stood outside.

The door quickly closed for a second and reopened wide. A tall, muscular man with broad shoulders brushed a hand through his grey hair. A smile touched his suntanned, wrinkled face before he stepped out and wrapped his arms around Mark, hugging him as a father would his son.

Stan pulled on the brake and switched off the engine. 'I think we've got the right place,' he said and got out.

Jane tentatively opened the back door and slipped out. She waited by the side of the car as Mark's father released him and quickly entered the house. Mark beckoned her and Stan to join him.

He entered the house and Jane followed him with Stan shutting the door behind them. They were in the main room, plainly decorated, which stretched the full length of the house from front to back. A fire was blazing away in a wood-burning stove, which was positioned against the left wall in front of a dark brown three seater sofa.

Images of a football match flashed on a muted television screen that was sitting on its stand, angled over the corner of the room next to the front window. On the back wall was an old dresser with two wooden chairs each side of it.

They were stood in a space between the back of the sofa and a folded table pushed up against the right wall.

Jane heard a gasp as a grey-haired, tall, slim woman hobbled through the only other door in the room just in front of them.

'Adrian,' she cried and stumbled into Mark's outstretched arms.

'Mom.'

His mother gripped him tightly as if she was afraid to let him go and Jane saw a smile of gratitude and relief on his father's face.

Mark gently uncurled his mother's arms from around him and took her hand.

'Mom, Dad, I want to introduce you to Jane and Stan.'

His mother swiftly used her free hand to wipe away tears that had appeared in her eyes and took Jane's extended hand. 'Hello, Jane. Adrian has told us all about you. I'm Maureen.'

Jane noticed the twang of a Yorkshire accent mixed with, what seemed, an American one. She smiled and nodded, frightened to say anything in case the emotions rising inside of her spilled out. She so missed her parents.

Stan stepped forward and shook Maureen's hand. 'I'm a friend,' he said as Maureen hesitated on what to say.

As soon as Stan had released Maureen's hand she pulled Mark over to the sofa.

Mark's father now stepped forward and shook Stan's hand, and when he took Jane's he smiled warmly and squeezed it. 'Eee, I've been looking forward to meeting thee, lass. Call me Jack.'

Jane nodded again and her words stumbled out in a hardly-heard whisper.

'Thank you.'

'Kettle's on. Sit thee sen down,' he said, indicating the sofa and wooden chairs.

Jane took the wooden chair closest to the fire and Stan sat on the other. She watched Mark nod and smile at his mother while she chattered to him non-stop. Jane didn't hear what was being said; her mind was trying to control the empty feelings that were creeping into her heart. A deep resonance of sadness she had suppressed since the death of her parents was beginning to overwhelm her. She thought she had overcome it, put the emotions safely under lock and key, but somehow the lock had broken open and everything inside was at risk of spilling out. It was taking all her reserve to hold them back.

A steaming ceramic mug appeared before her and she looked up to see Mark's father staring at her. He smiled quickly, almost apologetically. Perhaps he had caught a look on her face; she didn't know, but she took the cup from him and nodded in thanks. Then she focused all her attention on the hot fluid inside.

'You're not the same, any longer,' Mark's mother said, touching the very short, dark hair and moving the ponytail on Mark's head. 'But it's rite.' She nodded and took the mug Jack gave her.

'What about you, Mom, are you better? I noticed you're limping.'

'Don't you go fretting thee self now,' she replied, taking his hand.

Jack sat down on the other side of Mark and grunted, 'That poison is what's done it.'

Jane saw the look of horror on Mark's face and when he looked at his mother, she saw sadness wash over him.

'I'm so sorry.'

'Ee, lad, it wadn't your fault,' Jack replied.

Mark turned to his father, a touch of anger in his voice.

'It was; yes, it was. I brought this on you and I'm going to fix it.'

Mark's mother stared at him with a frightened look. 'What are thee thinking of?' she whispered.

Mark squeezed her hand. 'I'm going to see Ferrand. I'm going to stop this.'

His mother's face went pale and Jane felt her own stomach twitch.

'No, Ade, no,' his mother pleaded.

Mark shook his head. 'I have to do this. You can't keep hiding. I can't keep hiding. I want a normal life with someone I love.' He looked over to Jane.

Jane gave him a small smile, but inside, her stomach was squeezing her tighter.

'The lad needs to do what's best,' his father said and got up. He looked at Stan. 'There ain't room for all of thee.'

Stan waved the concern away. 'Sofa's good for me, sir, if you don't mind. Otherwise, I can find a hotel.'

Mark's father nodded. 'The sofa's mighty comfy.'

Then he turned to Jane. 'Spare room needs making up. Two pairs of hands are better than one.' He moved towards the side door.

Jane got up and followed him through a small kitchen to some stairs at the back of the house. At the top of the stairs was a small landing and three doors. Jack went through the first door, which was a large bedroom at the back of the house. Just inside was the airing cupboard and he passed Jane some bed linen. They moved out of the room into the next room which was the bedroom overlooking the road. It was just big enough to hold a double bed and small wardrobe.

Jack cleared his throat as he threw one end of the fitted

sheet across to Jane. 'Thank you for helping our Adrian when he needed it most.'

Jane looked at him, puzzled, and slipped the end of the sheet over the mattress.

'He had nowt and was lonely,' Jack sighed. 'I saw it in his emails. He missed having someone he could trust and talk to.'

'It must have been a strain on all of you,' Jane said softly, finishing the other end of the sheet.

Jack nodded and a touch of sadness caught in his eyes. 'Aye, more Maureen than me. She wouldna show it to any of thee, but what happened to her was…' He trailed off.

Jane cut in. 'Mark… sorry, I mean Adrian was beside himself when he found out she was ill.'

'Aye, lass, that he'd be.' He waited until Jane had finished putting on the pillowcases before he said, 'You make thee self at home. No need to ask; just help yourself to anything you want.'

'Thank you,' Jane said, focusing on putting the duvet in the cover.

They placed it on the bed and stood back. 'Job's a goodun,' Jack said, smiling.

Jane felt the warmth from his smile and saw a fondness sparkle in his eyes. He radiated a kindness so much like her own father had when he was alive. She smiled back and they returned downstairs.

★ ★ ★

That evening Maureen cooked them a beef roast dinner. They all squeezed around the table. Even Stan, who had been going to go to the local pub, but for Maureen's insistence he stay to taste her Yorkshire puddings. The conversation was light over dinner, but when the dessert of bread and butter pudding came, Mark suddenly said, 'Tell me what happened when you became ill, Mom?'

His mother shook her head. 'It's nowt you need to worry about.'

'But I want to know.' He looked at his dad.

'Aye, lad, that you do. Your mother got ill after she'd been shopping. Someone knocked into her and she collapsed in the street.'

Jane listened, but wasn't sure she wanted to hear this.

He continued, 'It was the start of cancer, they said.'

Maureen gave a short whimper, the memory obviously still painful to her.

Jack took her hand. 'We believed it, no reason to doubt t'doctor.'

'Then I asked you to get a second opinion,' Mark contributed.

'Yes, lad, you did. We called Dr Jules, the family doctor. He came to the hospital and checked your mother's chart and tests.' Jack took a breath and Jane could see his face was flushing with anger. 'There was nowt wrong with her, except the stuff they'd been giving her.' He swallowed hard and regained his composure. 'That doctor at the hospital was poisoning her with the treatment he said she needed.'

Maureen squeezed his hand. 'The doctor disappeared when we called the police. The hospital said he was a locum, but couldn't trace him.'

Jane placed her hand over her mouth. She couldn't believe what she was hearing.

'When Maureen was well enough, we came back to England. We needed to go somewhere even Ferrand couldn't find us. No one knew of this place except you, Adrian.' He paused and looked at Jane and Stan to explain. 'This belongs to a friend of ours and can't be traced to us.'

Mark sighed deeply; his whole body sagged in the seat. Jane touched his leg and squeezed it when he looked at her. There was guilt in his eyes.

He turned back to his parents. 'I had no idea it would come to this; I'm so sorry.'

'There's no good blaming thee sen,' his mother said positively. 'We're here now, together.' She smiled. 'Eat, before your pudding gets cold.'

They ate in silence. Jane watched Mark almost force the food into his mouth. He put his spoon down and turned to his father. 'What about the children?'

His father stopped eating. 'When your mother took ill, Solita disappeared with the children.'

'Were… were they okay?'

'Aye, lad, they were.' Mark's father got up and went to the dresser. When he returned he handed a photo to Mark. 'This is the most up-to-date photo we have.'

Mark took the photo and his hand shook.

Jane could see the top half of two young children. A boy with short, spiky, blond hair was standing stiffly to attention, his shoulders pulled back and his head pushed forward. He was smiling as if he was pleased with himself. Jane could see Mark's features in his face. Next to the boy was a little girl, younger than the boy. She had blonde hair in ringlets around her face and was grasping a fluffy toy rabbit to her chest. She looked like the sweetest child Jane had ever seen, and when grown up would have men fighting over her.

Mark's body shuddered as he traced his finger over the children's faces. Jane could see the effort it was taking to keep his emotions inside.

'You… you don't know where they've gone?'

His father shook his head. 'I keep checking my emails, just in case she gets in contact, but…' He left the sentence unfinished.

'If you give me her description and where she last lived, I might be able to help,' Stan said, rising from his chair. He put a hand on Mark's shoulder. 'I'm sure Ferrand hasn't got them,' he said.

'How do you know?'

'He'd have made Solita get in contact by now.'

Mark heaved in a deep breath. 'Do what you can, please.'

Stan nodded.

Mark suddenly got up. 'I'm going to bed,' he said quietly.

His mother went to him and hugged him. 'Goodnight, and don't you worry too much.'

Mark kissed her on the cheek and left the room.

A few minutes later Jane made her own excuses and followed him. Outside the bedroom door she heard him muttering. She felt a heaviness in her chest, and tears came as she thought about how he must be feeling.

When she heard him sniff and blow his nose, she gently opened the door. He looked up from where he was sitting on the bed and she saw sadness in his eyes. She went straight to him, drawing him into her arms. He hugged her tightly, his breath warm against her neck. They didn't speak; there was no need for words.

That night they lay in each other's arms, awake. Jane nestled her head into his shoulder. 'What happened to make you leave your children? Were you still in America?' she asked softly.

There was a moment of silence before Mark said, 'Yes, we lived in Ohio and my parents didn't live too far away from us.

As you know, Solita and I had a massive argument when she found out I had destroyed the crystal and all my work.'

'Did you burn all your notes?'

'Yes, everything. The next morning she didn't speak to me.' Mark's mind returned to the day after the row…

* * *

He was in the kitchen making his own breakfast when he heard Solita in the hallway. He moved to the door and caught sight of her back as she and the children went out of the front door. She glanced back at him, not saying a word, as the front door shut behind her.

Mark returned to his breakfast, rubbing the small of his back. The sofa wasn't the most comfortable thing to spend the night on. He ate his breakfast without really tasting the food, then got in the car and drove to work.

He tried as hard as he could to concentrate on what he was doing, but his mind kept reliving the events of the previous day. The destruction of – what he believed was the most significant invention the world would ever know – the master crystal that could generate unlimited energy. He had had no choice but to destroy it, for its pureness had been too easily manipulated into something destructive.

'Call for you, Adrian, a Mr Ferrand.'

Mark looked over to his colleague, shaking his head. This was the fourth call and he had only been at work for three hours. The man was persistent beyond belief. There was no way he would allow anyone to have the knowledge to build the crystal now. It was just too dangerous.

Mark put down what he was doing, removed his lab coat and tossed it onto the hooks by the door.

His colleague, who had taken the call, glanced up at him. 'What's up?'

'Family problems. I'm going home. Can you cover for me?' His colleague nodded and Mark left the building.

It was lunchtime and he knew Solita would be home. When he walked through the front door, she was just coming out of the bathroom with Sophie in her arms.

'What are you doing here?' she asked, startled.

Mark felt the bitterness in her voice. 'This is my home too,' he grunted as he passed her and went into the lounge.

His son was playing in the playpen and as soon as he saw Mark, a smile came on his face. He lifted his arms to be picked up. Mark felt his annoyance fall away. 'Does my Jamie want to come for a walk with Daddy?'

The boy excitedly stamped his feet and when Mark picked him up, his son grabbed him around the neck and nuzzled into his face. Mark was so filled with a rush of happiness, he planted a big kiss on Jamie's forehead.

The boy wriggled with excitement and Mark carried him into the hall to get his coat. More giggles of pleasure followed as Jamie pushed his arm through his coat sleeve.

Solita came out of the bedroom with Sophie in her arms. 'What the hell are you doing?' she shouted.

The boy stopped laughing and shivered.

'I'm taking Jamie out in his pushchair,' Mark answered, swinging his son down into the buggy. He smiled smugly to himself, knowing that Solita would be annoyed at his use of Jamie instead of her preferred name of James.

Solita shot across to him and grabbed his arm. 'No, you can't,' she yelled.

Jamie's bottom lip began to quiver and he looked worryingly at Solita.

'Why?' Mark demanded.

Solita hesitated, then said, 'I'm taking them to my mother's.'

Mark frowned. 'But Sophie's just had her bath and is due her nap, isn't she?'

Solita glared at him with such fury that Mark almost stepped back, but he held his ground.

'Don't you ever tell me how to look after my kids,' she spat. 'You're so selfish, you think of only yourself. Well, I've had enough of it. I want a divorce.'

Mark couldn't move. His body had become numb. He stared at her, not wanting to acknowledge what she had said.

Jamie began to cry, and then Sophie started too, hesitant at first as if not sure why she should be crying at all.

Solita pushed Mark hard in the chest. 'Get out and don't come back!'

Mark stepped backwards in shock, his body still not responding, his mind overwhelmed with what was happening. 'Solita,' he blurted out.

'GET OUT!' she screamed above the crying of the two children.

Mark automatically turned, opened the front door and left. He shuffled to his car in a daze, found his keys in his pocket and got in. He sat there, staring at the steering wheel. *What now?*

He stared at the keys in his hand. It took a minute before he put them in the ignition and started the car. Finally, he reversed out of the driveway and drove down the road. He had no idea where he was going or what he should do.

His life had been happy, hadn't it? He'd always provided for his family, so why had Solita got so upset? Surely, it couldn't have anything to do with him destroying the crystal and his work. It didn't make sense.

He stopped the car and thought about going back, getting a proper answer from her, but decided not to and drove on. Soon, he was pulling into the drive of his parents' house. How he got there he didn't know or remember. He sat in the car and waited. It would be hours before they returned from work.

It was a knock on the car window that brought him back from wherever he had been. He didn't know or remember anything of the last three hours. He saw his mother's concerned face at the window and opened the door.

'What is it?' she asked. 'What's happened?'

He couldn't speak; the image of Solita shouting at him numbed his words.

'Is it the children?' she persisted, her hand on his arm.

He shook his head.

'The lad's in shock,' his father said. 'Let's get inside.'

Mark felt his mother take his arm and guide him into the house and into the kitchen. She gently pushed him down onto a chair and sat next to him. 'Put kettle on,' she said to his father.

Instead, a tumbler filled with whisky was placed in front of him. Mark downed it in one and saw the look of disapproval on his mother's face as his father filled it again. The warm spirit slid down Mark's throat like nectar, awakening the muscles that had paralysed his speech. The fluid slid into his stomach, filling the emptiness inside. 'Solita chucked me out,' he blurted. 'She wants a divorce.' He downed the remaining liquid and waited for his father to fill the glass again.

'Jack, don't you think that's enough?' his mother said reproachfully.

'The lad's in need of it, hun,' he said.

'She says it's my fault,' Mark said quickly.

'She would,' his mother retorted. 'Nothing ever pleases her.'

Mark drank the third whisky, feeling it swamp the hollowness in his body and send a comforting tingling of confidence into his head. He slammed the glass down hard onto the table, making his mother jump. 'I'm going back. Who the hell… does she think she is…?' He stood up abruptly and paused as the spinning in his head blurred his vision. He felt his father's hands land firmly on his shoulders, forcing him back down on the chair.

'Aye, son; it's your house, but go back like this and she'll have you in jail.'

Mark felt the anger drain away and stared at the glass. His father filled it again and this time Mark took a sip. 'What am I going to do?' he pleaded with his father.

His father sat on the other side of him and squeezed his shoulder. 'Your mother will fix you some food and after a night's rest, you and I are going to forge a plan to go to court.'

★ ★ ★

'And that's what happened,' Mark said. 'Dad got a good lawyer and I got contact rights.'

'But what happened to Ferrand?' Jane asked.

'The man had the nerve to call me at my parents' house. He wouldn't take no for an answer.'

'So how come you left America and came to Jersey?'

Mark closed his eyes. It was still painful and he replied, 'I left to protect my family.' He could see Jane was anxious to learn more, so he continued, 'It was after the court had awarded me the rights to see the children...'

★ ★ ★

Mark was outside the courtroom with his parents and his lawyer. The court had given him the children every other weekend and once in the week, plus alternate Christmases and New Year.

Solita came out of the court and stormed towards him. Her words were blistering. 'If you think this is finished, think again!'

Mark was calm. 'They are my children; I want to see them.'

'You can't see them. I don't want you to have anything to do with them. They are MY children.'

Mark could feel his anger rising, but he swallowed it back, forcing himself to remain relaxed. 'The court has made an order. There's nothing you can do.'

Solita's eyes blazed into him. 'We'll see about that!' she screeched and marched away.

Mark turned back to his parents and his father smiled. 'Well handled, lad.'

★ ★ ★

Within a week Mark got a call from Ferrand, but he refused to speak to him. He was trying to bring some normality back to his life. The maintenance payment to Solita allowed her to remain in the house and still gave him enough to find a place to rent, although his parents had suggested he not rush to move out.

On the Friday evening, a week after the court case, Mark

decided to go to the local bar and have a night out, giving his parents some personal time, although they never complained about him being there. In fact, he knew his mother was enjoying it. This weekend they were going to prepare the spare room for when Jamie and Sophie came the following weekend, but Mark was really looking forward to this coming Wednesday. He had taken the day off work to take the children out and was prepared for a battle with Solita when he went to pick them up, but he knew she couldn't stop him.

The cab dropped him off in the quiet and dimly lit street a few yards from the bar's side door. His mind was so busy going over the plans he had made for the children's day out that he didn't see the red Cadillac pull up onto the pavement in front of him. A tall, broad man got out and blocked his path. Mark moved to pass him, but the man's gorilla-like hand slammed into his chest, sending him backwards a few steps.

Mark looked at him warily. The man was massive, standing taller than him and almost twice as wide. His bald head emphasised the sharp features of his tough-looking face and his thickset neck merged with his broad shoulders.

'Mr Ferrand wants to see you,' said a thin, whiny voice from the other side of the car.

Mark turned and saw a tall, lanky man with a pointed face leaning against the driver's open door.

'Tell Ferrand to get lost. I'm not interested.'

The bald man caught and twisted Mark's arm up behind his back, causing him to yell out in pain.

The lanky man smiled. 'But Mr Ferrand insists.'

Mark tried to push back from the car's rear door, but the grip on his arm cancelled out any countermove with more pain. Desperately, he looked towards the bar, hoping someone would come out and see them, but the street remained empty.

With a hard shove, Mark was pushed into the rear of the car. Once his arm was released, he slipped across the seat to open the other door, but as he reached it, the barrel of a gun slammed hard against his temple, forcing him back into the seat.

The lanky man shook his head. 'Nah, I wouldn't try it.'

Mark carefully turned towards the front; the man was grinning at him. He wondered if he should risk going anyway, knowing they didn't want him dead, but the moment had passed, for the bald man was in the car with a hand on his shoulder.

The lanky man turned back to the wheel and drove them away.

'Where're we going?' Mark demanded, hoping his voice showed strength and not the nervous fear that was wrenching in his stomach.

'A hotel room,' the lanky man said. 'You should consider yourself lucky,' he continued conversationally. 'Mr Ferrand never meets anyone in person. Even we haven't seen him.' He paused as if waiting for Mark to respond, but Mark kept quiet, so he added, 'Or maybe it's not so lucky you see him.' He sniggered.

They arrived at an obscure hotel in a rundown area of Ohio. One of those seedy places where people usually get killed in the movies. Mark wondered if this was going to be the place of his death, but he didn't think so. Ferrand wanted something he now only had in his head, so killing him was not an option; but getting the information from him was another thing and he was not relishing the methods Ferrand might use to get it.

As soon as the car stopped, the bald man grabbed Mark's

arms, squeezing them against his chest so tightly Mark caught his breath. The lanky man got out and opened the rear door, indicating with the gun that Mark should exit. Mark got out and with the bald man's massive hand at the back of his neck, he was forced up the stairs of the hotel to the second floor. At room 204, Mark was made to face the door while the lanky man knocked three times. After a minute he opened the door and pushed Mark inside. The door quickly closed, leaving Mark in total darkness. He stood for a moment, adjusting his eyes to the dim light.

A light came on in the far corner by the window. It was the bedside light and a man dressed in dark trousers and a white shirt was sitting on a wooden chair next to it. Mark guessed he was in his early sixties, as the thick, dark, short hair had a hint of white at the front and down the sides. It was pushed back from a high forehead, exposing a face that was well tanned with wrinkles collecting around narrow, sharp eyes.

The man leaned his slim body forward so that his elbows rested on his knees. 'Mr Stevenson, at last,' he said, his voice soft, but controlled.

Mark couldn't contain his annoyance any longer. 'I told you I wasn't interested; nothing has changed.'

'Ah, you think so?' A smile briefly touched his thin lips. He beckoned Mark in.

Mark walked to the edge of the bed and stopped. 'What do you want?' he asked, his voice steady.

'I want the crystal you produced. Solita told me it generates perpetual energy.'

'Solita is wrong,' Mark countered.

Ferrand leaned back into the wooden chair and slipped his hand into his trouser pocket. He drew out what looked like a photo and threw it on the bed.

Mark leaned forward and picked it up. His eyes widened as he saw his crystal shining with an enormous bright light. 'How...?' He didn't finish, knowing immediately that it could have only been Solita.

'I want it and you will give it to me,' Ferrand said smoothly.

Mark thought quickly; had Solita told him it had been destroyed? 'I haven't got it... with me,' he said, looking down to the bedcover.

Ferrand leapt over the bed and pushed him up against the wall. One massive hand tightly squeezed Mark's neck while the other turned into a fist and thudded into his chest.

Mark gasped in shock, momentarily caught off guard, but he quickly recovered and pushed his hands into Ferrand's face.

Ferrand hit him again harder, this time in the stomach.

Mark doubled up in agony, forcing his body from the wall.

Ferrand's hand tightened its hold on Mark's throat and pushed him back.

Mark struggled to breathe. He grasped at Ferrand's hand, trying to force it away from his throat, but Ferrand was too strong. He began to choke in his own saliva and his eyes were bulging from their sockets. Ferrand drew closer and he could see the coldness behind the startling blue eyes.

'Don't play with me, Adrian,' he whispered viciously. 'Solita told me you destroyed it.'

The pressure on his throat eased a bit, allowing him to swallow and gulp in air.

'You are going to make me another one,' Ferrand said softly.

The hand suddenly tightened again and as Mark began to lose consciousness, he heard, 'Or watch your family suffer.'

Mark came to, hanging between the bald and lanky man. They were half carrying, half dragging him down the stairs. His mind was fuzzy, his vision struggling to clear as they reached the car. He groaned as he fell onto the back seat and gently touched his throat. It was really sore and painful.

The bald man got in beside him and smirked at Mark's discomfort. Then the car was moving at speed and it wasn't long before it stopped again. The bald man roughly dragged him out and onto the pavement. They were back at the bar where they had taken him from. The lanky man grinned into Mark's face.

'You have a week,' he said, admiring the bruising skin on Mark's neck. 'We'll contact you; we know where to find you.' He poked Mark hard in the chest with a bony finger. 'Don't be late.' He twisted away sharply and both men returned to the car and drove off.

Mark stared at the spot where the car had been. His body was trembling and his skin felt clammy. Sickness swelled in his stomach as he realised he was in deep trouble.

★ ★ ★

'What did you do?' Jane gasped.

'I told my parents I was going to give Ferrand the crystal. It was the easiest thing to do to protect them, Solita and the children.'

'So what happened?'

Mark took a deep breath. 'My father said I couldn't trust a man like that and something the lanky man said that night, made me realise that he was right. Even if I handed it over I wouldn't be safe, nor would my family.' Mark sighed. 'I really screwed it up for everyone, didn't I?'

'No, it was Solita who screwed it up.'

'Anyway, my parents made arrangements to disappear to somewhere on the west coast of America. They closed their bank accounts, left their jobs without notice and took only a few belongings in a bag as they knew we were being watched. Luckily, the house was only rented; otherwise, it would have been much more difficult.'

'Oh my God, that must have been such an upheaval. What about Solita?'

'I called her and told her Ferrand would harm her and the children if she didn't disappear. I said I wanted her and the children safe before I did anything. I... I told her I would not contact her after this call or try to see the children and that my father would keep funding the maintenance payments to her.'

'What did she say?'

'Good.'

'Good?' Jane was shocked.

'I didn't realise it at the time, but that was exactly what she wanted.' Mark stopped as if his throat had clogged up.

'Why didn't you go to the police?'

'I did, but I didn't have sufficient information to give them, did I? The name Ferrand didn't come up in any database; I didn't know where he lived or the registration of the car his thugs used.' Mark sighed deeply. 'The only way was for all of us to go into hiding and even that didn't work, as he found my mother. I just hope he hasn't found Solita and the children.'

Jane took his hand and squeezed it. 'Don't worry; we'll find your children. I'm sure they're okay.'

CHAPTER SEVEN

Stan shook his head as he hung up on the call he had just received. He turned to Mark, who was sitting on the sofa with his mother.

'All I can tell you is that Solita's in Arizona, somewhere.'

Mark sighed. 'You did your best. So what do we do now?'

'We send out an SOS, lad,' his father said, entering from the kitchen with the laptop in his hand. 'I've sent a message to her old email address. I'm sure she'd not have disconnected it. It's her only lifeline to your money.'

Jane looked at him from her seat by the dresser. 'I don't understand.'

'Adrian may have disappeared from their lives, but he didn't want the children to suffer, so we arranged for me to send Solita his money. This is the email I used to confirm payment had been sent.' He looked pleased with himself. 'I've just told her there's a problem wit' money and can she contact me.'

Stan nodded admiringly. 'You're a devious man, Mr Stevenson; I like it.' He paused then said, 'Maybe I can trace where the bank sends the money, but it may take a while to contact my specialist.'

Jane turned to look at him. 'Is there anything you can't do, Stan?'

He thought for a bit. 'Not much.'

Mark's father tapped the laptop with his fingers. 'Let's see if the email works before you call your friend, and please call me Jack.'

★ ★ ★

A day later, Mark's father came into the lounge, smiling. 'I've heard from Solita,' he announced, triumphantly. 'I've told her you need to urgently see her and the children. That t'would be in her best interest if she meets you.'

'And?' Mark asked, hesitantly.

'She's agreed to a meeting. She's in Tucson. I have her address.'

'Yes! Good work, Dad.' Mark turned to Stan and was about to say something when he stopped.

Jane saw him frown and wondered what was wrong.

'I'll make the travel arrangements,' Stan said, reaching into his jacket pocket.

Mark hesitated. 'Ah, c… can you just wait a bit?'

Stan looked up from his phone.

Mark cleared his throat. 'I just need to do something first.'

Jane looked at him, puzzled by his behaviour.

He avoided making eye contact with her, then said, 'Can I have a word with you, Jane?'

Her stomach clenched as he came over and gently took her hand. She knew something was up and it involved her. He led her through the kitchen and out of the back door, into the small garden. The sun was out, but it was bitterly cold, so he went back inside and returned with their coats.

Jane's senses were on high alert. She knew he was going to tell her something she wasn't going to like and her body was tensing itself for the blow.

He helped her with her coat before slowly putting on his. The zip seemed to be stuck as he tried to do it up and he fiddled with it, wandering over to the little stone wall which enclosed the small lawn.

Jane couldn't stand the wait any longer and blurted out, 'You're leaving me!'

Mark turned round; his face looked penitent. 'I want you to be safe.'

She stared at him as her body went into meltdown, sending a shudder of terror into her heart. 'I… I can't stay. I need to… I have to come with you,' she mumbled.

Mark came over and put his arms around her. 'My parents have agreed you can stay with them,' he whispered.

Jane pushed him away. 'You've discussed this with your parents before even talking to me!'

Mark stepped back, surprised at her reaction. 'I… I didn't think you—'

'How dare you!' Jane shouted, cutting him off. 'I've been with you every step of the way and you didn't even think about asking me what I wanted!'

Mark moved towards her, his arms open. 'Jane, I— '

'You're not leaving me!' she cried, her anger forcing tears to her eyes. 'You're not…'

Mark pulled her into his body and held her tight. 'I didn't mean to hurt you. I love you so much; I just want you to be safe.'

Jane couldn't stop the tears overwhelming her and she buried her head into his shoulder and cried.

'Please, Jane; stay here.'

She shook her head, unable to speak.

'Please, Jane; don't be like this. I need to know those I love are safe before I see Ferrand.'

Jane lifted her head, tears slipping down her cheeks. 'You… you don't understand. I can't…' She paused, hardening her voice. 'I won't stay behind.'

Mark gripped her firmly on the upper arms and pushed

her away from his body. His face was touched with anger. 'I'm not arguing with you on this. I don't want you with me.' A ripple of regret touched his mouth at the harshness of his words.

Jane saw it and capitalised on it. 'That's okay; you can leave me behind, but you can't stop me from following you.'

Mark half-turned away, flinging his arms up in frustration. 'What IS the matter with you? This isn't going to be any picnic, you know. You could die!'

Jane grabbed his arm and roughly turned him back to face her. 'And you don't know what it's like to have those you love leave you and never come back.' The memory of her parents, storming out of the house, filled her mind and fresh tears came.

'You don't know what it feels like living with the guilt of letting them go and not being there to save them.' She let go of his arm and looked away. 'I was left alone; I had no one left to love me.' She looked back to his face, a blurry image through her tears. 'I don't want to be left alone again.'

He pulled her close, his arms around her.

A stillness swept over the garden. The chilled air froze, the light wind vanished and the birds were silent.

After a few moments Mark put his hands on each side of her face and kissed her tenderly. When he drew back, he gently wiped away the wetness under her eyes. 'I'm so sorry. I had no idea.'

'Please don't leave me.'

Mark kissed her forehead gently. 'Can't have you getting into trouble by yourself now, can I? I suppose you'd better stick with us, where I can keep an eye on you.'

Jane hugged him tightly. 'Thank you, thank you,' she whispered.

'Yes, well, you may regret this decision,' he murmured.

'I won't as long as I'm with you.' She eased away and wiped all remaining tears from her eyes. 'I think I better go and freshen up.' She smiled and gave him a peck on the lips before going back into the house.

In the bathroom, she washed the tear stains from her face and tied back her hair before going into the bedroom. She slumped down onto the bed, suddenly exhausted.

The feelings she had for Mark seemed overwhelming and it was as if something deep and old was connecting her to him. She'd never experienced that before in any other relationship. There was also something disturbing about the terror she felt just now. Could her need to be with him stem from the loss of her parents?

She was so focused on her thoughts she didn't hear Mark enter the bedroom until he sat down next to her. She smiled at him.

'Are you feeling all right?' he asked softly.

'Yes. I didn't realise how much the death of my parents had affected me.'

'What happened to them?'

Jane sighed.

'If it's too painful to talk about it, I'll understand,' Mark said quickly.

Jane took hold of his hand. 'It's okay. I need to do this.' She reached into her pocket and found the pebble Lola had given her. 'I need to release the emotion and see my parents differently.'

Mark frowned.

'Lola said the stone people help us release toxic energies that we keep in our bodies when we bury our emotions. She gave me this stone so I could release the emotions I had suppressed when my parents died.'

Mark nodded in understanding. 'Lola was quite special, wasn't she?'

Jane smiled, remembering Lola's childlike innocence that had underpinned her wonderful wisdom. 'I miss her.'

After a moment of silence, Jane continued, 'When my friend died in the boat accident, I wouldn't go in or near a motorboat again. I was terrified.'

'I'm not surprised,' Mark said, rubbing her hand.

'A couple of years later my parents and I were invited to go on their friend's boat to Granville for the day, to do some shopping and have lunch. I refused to go and begged my parents not to go either. We had a huge row over it. But they went and never came back.'

'What happened to them?'

'The police enquiry discovered they had got to Granville and left later that afternoon. They believed the boat went off course on the way back to Jersey and crashed on the rocks of Chausey.' Jane stopped speaking, her emotions stirring up inside her.

'How did it happen? I mean, what caused it to crash?'

Her voice quivered when she spoke. 'Witnesses at the port told police they saw my parents' friend drinking wine, alone, at the bar after lunch and later they saw him staggering along the pontoon towards the boat.' Jane swallowed and cleared her throat. 'They were surprised when they saw him take the boat out of the marina.'

She gripped the pebble in her hand tighter. 'My parents didn't know anything about boats… They had no idea…' She stopped talking, choked by the raging anger inside.

Mark squeezed her hand and she looked at him.

'He should have looked after them… He shouldn't have drunk…' She pressed her lips together, forcing it back, but it had come too far and it thundered out. 'It was his fault they died... HIS FAULT!' Tears burst into her eyes and she heaved in a breath. 'He took them from me. Took everything I loved from me. He had NO right to do that. NO RIGHT. I HATE HIM!' Jane took a deep breath and blew all her anger and hate into the stone. The more she blew into the stone, the lighter her body became. Finally, she stopped blowing and took a breath. There was no more anger left and she sat quietly.

'There was nothing you could have done, Jane.'

She looked at Mark with irritation. Another emotion was filling the space the anger had left. 'I should have gone with them... I might have been able to stop their friend from drinking so much or... or I could have stopped my parents from getting back on his boat... If I hadn't been so stubborn... If only I had gone...' Jane blew again into the stone; this time it was her regret.

'It was my fault, my stupid fear of boats. I could have saved them, I could have...' The tears cascaded down her face and she sobbed into the stone; all her guilt, all her sorrow. As soon as that had gone, more anger came, this time towards herself. It had been her actions that had set the events in motion. She blew long and hard into the stone until all her breath was gone. She gave a big sigh.

'It wasn't your fault,' Mark said quietly. 'Your parents made the decision to go.'

Jane stared at him. 'You're right. They left me. They knew I was scared of boats, yet they still went. They shouldn't have gone! They abandoned me!' Her throat clogged up and she quickly blew into the stone the anger towards her parents she didn't realise she had.

After the last breath she felt strangely empty and cold; it

was as if the emotions around her parents' death had been a heavy mass held inside her body, keeping her a prisoner of their fateful memory. She remembered what Lola had told her about releasing her emotions and how to allow herself to give and receive forgiveness so that she would remember her parents with love. She took a moment to hold forgiveness for the friend of her parents, for her parents and finally for herself. It was only after she had done this that she felt an enormous flood of warmth and love wash through her.

She thought about her parents, recalling them in her mind and this time she only saw memories of their happy, smiling faces.

Mark was looking at her intently. 'What just happened?'

'I think I have just released myself from the effects of the past. I'm now remembering my parents with love, not sadness.' She held up the pebble. 'Lola was so right about this.'

Mark put his arm around her shoulders. 'You're looking much better.'

Jane hugged him tightly; she felt fantastic, so peaceful and loving. She kissed him gently on the lips before getting up. 'I have to bury this pebble in the garden so it can be cleansed by the earth, then I'll start packing. When are we going?'

Mark smiled. 'Not for a few days. My parents would love us to spend Christmas with them. If that's okay with you?'

'It's Christmas already? I didn't even know. I always had such fun at Christmas with my parents. My dad used to hide the presents…' She stopped. 'Oh my God, this is the first time since they died that I have remembered that. I never really let myself enjoy Christmas after their deaths because I always felt sad they weren't with me.'

She smiled warmly at Mark's concerned face. 'It's okay.

Wow, I feel so differently now. I think this Christmas will be wonderful.'

She saw him relax. 'I expect you haven't spent Christmas with your parents for years either.'

'No, I haven't, so it will be nice; but it's even better with you here.'

Jane couldn't stop smiling; her mouth seemed fixed in a permanent grin. 'And what about Stan, is he joining us?'

'No, he says he's going to have Christmas with Fiona. On the condition we don't leave here, or contact anyone.'

Jane couldn't imagine Stan celebrating Christmas in the usual traditional way; she couldn't picture him pulling crackers or sitting on the sofa watching TV after a huge lunch. But if he was spending it with Fiona, then maybe he would be doing just that.

CHAPTER EIGHT

The flight from Manchester to Phoenix took nearly fifteen hours and Stan drove the Ford Fiesta hire car out of Phoenix airport onto Highway 10 towards Tucson at 7pm. The motel they had booked for the night was only twenty-three minutes from the airport, but even so, Jane couldn't stop herself from dozing on the backseat.

As soon as she closed her eyes she was in the meadow by the forest where she usually met her spirit guides, Three Wolves and Spirit Wind. It had been a while since her last meditation and she was excited to see them again.

She looked around and saw Three Wolves standing in his usual place by the entrance to the forest. His appearance hadn't changed since her last meeting with him, with his leather trousers over moccasin shoes and a thin leather shirt adorned with a string of bones and feathers. On his head and sitting on top of his long, thick, black hair was a band with a single feather.

But there was something different about him this time, something about his manner. She thought no more of it and walked over to him, smiling. 'It's good to see you again,' she said.

He didn't smile back, which was strange. Instead, he greeted her with a serious look.

'What is it?' she asked, getting a little worried.

'There is danger, Jane. You must be careful.'

She acknowledged his words with a head nod. 'I know, but we have Stan with us.'

Three Wolves frowned. 'There is much you do not know and much is hidden from you. You will need to be on your guard. Ancient events are rising.'

'What do you mean? What ancient events?'

'Past lives are converging. This will be the lifetime to change the outcome or face destruction.'

Jane stared at him. 'What do you mean? Tell me what's going to happen.'

Three Wolves shook his head sadly. 'I cannot, for I know only a small part of what it is. Spirit Wind will show you, but not now. First, you must face the danger ahead.'

'Is it to do with Mark?'

He nodded.

Jane felt her breath catch in her throat. 'Wh...What...?' She couldn't get the words out. It was as if she didn't want to say them or hear the answer.

He took her hand and squeezed it. 'Have courage. Be alert; trust no one.'

Jane half heard the words for her mind was flashing images of all the possible things that could happen to Mark and each time it ended badly. She pushed her emotions back, forcing away the fear that was gripping her.

Three Wolves looked up as if he had heard something. 'It is time for you to go.' He turned and began to walk away.

'What do I do?' Jane cried out.

He looked back. 'You will know. Do not give in to fear. You are stronger than you think.' He smiled and walked into the forest.

A sudden jolt brought Jane back to the car and she saw that they had pulled off the road into the motel.

Stan stopped the car outside the reception and turned off the engine. 'I'll check us in,' he said and got out.

Mark turned round from the front seat to face her. 'Are you okay?'

Jane nodded.

'You don't look okay,' Mark pressed.

'I've had a message from Three Wolves. We must be careful and stay alert.'

'Anything else?'

Jane hesitated then said, 'He said ancient events were rising and something about change the outcome or face destruction.'

Mark suddenly looked worried.

'What is it?' she said, leaning forward.

'It's the universal power, it must be. I think he's warning me not to use it.' He paused then looked at her with determination. 'Ever since I first brought it into existence, I've known and kind of sensed that I mustn't do it again. Africa was the exception and even then you saw how destructive it can be. I promise you, Jane, I won't let Ferrand have it. It doesn't matter what he does, I won't give it to him.'

Just then Stan opened the door and got in. He must have sensed the atmosphere. 'I miss something?'

Jane shook her head and sat back. Mark's words were spinning around in her head.

'I've got us two rooms, number five and six so they are next to each other.' Stan started the car and drove to the parking area in front of the accommodation.

Jane got out of the car in a daze and took the key from Stan to room five. She sensed him staring at her, but she was too busy thinking about what Mark had said to respond.

Mark seemed so determined to stop Ferrand and she wondered how far he would truly go. In her visit to Three Wolves the images in her mind of what could happen to him had shown he went all the way to his death. She didn't want to accept that. She couldn't accept that. There had to be another way because she wasn't prepared to lose him.

She opened the room door and Mark carried their rucksacks in.

Stan remained at the open door. 'I suggest you call your ex from the public phone at reception and arrange a time to meet her at her house tomorrow. You will need to allow a couple of hours' drive to get there. Don't tell her where you are. Don't stay on the phone more than a minute. I'm going to freshen up and we'll order in something to eat.'

Jane could feel Stan's stare again, so she looked up and forced a smile. 'Okay, see you in an hour, then.'

He said nothing, just nodded and closed the door.

Jane flopped across the bed, exhausted, her mind focusing on the wrench in her stomach every time she thought about what lay ahead. Maybe she should have stayed with Mark's parents, but she knew that wasn't what she was meant to do, no matter how scared she was.

The bed moved and Mark lay next to her. He turned and put his arm over her body while gently kissing her cheek. He whispered softly, 'It's going to be all right.'

Jane snuggled into his body and thought, *But what if it isn't?*

★ ★ ★

The next morning they set off after breakfast to drive to Tucson. Jane tugged at the bottom of her cream blouse and pulled it further down over her light tan trousers. These were the only decent clothes she had brought with her; suitable for the weather, but meeting Mark's ex? She flicked bits of fluff from her handbag and twisted the strap around her fingers. She wasn't sure she wanted to or should meet Solita, nor what sort of reception she would get from this woman if she did meet her.

She could hear Mark chatting away to Stan in the front. He had been speaking almost non-stop since they had got up. She knew he was nervous, but also excited to see his children again.

Jane turned her focus to outside the car window. The weather was beautiful, with bright sunshine and clear blue skies. The air temperature was a comfortable 25 degrees centigrade.

The highway from Phoenix was huge with six lanes going in their direction and flyovers crossing above them with amazing names such as Superstition Springs Boulevard. Everything was oversized, even their cars, with Dodge Ram pick-up trucks flying past, their wheels as tall as the hire car itself. As the highway reduced to three lanes, the Catalina Mountains appeared before them. Jane couldn't believe how beautiful they were even at a distance and the closer they got, the more magnificent they became.

Solita lived just on the outskirts of Tucson at the base of the Catalina Mountains in a small housing complex. The estate was surrounded by dry desert and there was nothing to see for miles except the mountains. Stan drove through the estate twice, checking roads and exit points. Solita's house was at the end of one of the exit roads with her garden facing the open desert. Stan drove up to the house and stopped the car just past the drive where a black Chevrolet was parked.

Mark looked at Stan, then Jane. 'Well, I…'

'It's all right, Mark,' Jane said softly. 'I'll stop here with Stan. That way you don't have to worry about me and your ex-wife.'

There was relief on his face, but before he could get out of the car, Stan caught his arm and said, 'I think it's best you both go in.'

Mark was puzzled. 'Why?'

Stan hesitated.

Jane was surprised to see him hesitate again. He was normally so sure about everything.

Stan immediately sat taller, his voice was controlled. 'I'm going to park some distance away as I don't want to alarm your ex or your kids. It would be better not to tell your ex I'm here. If Jane goes in with you she can give you moral support.'

Jane stared at him. It didn't seem to make sense, but she trusted him and knew there must be a good reason for it. She got out of the car at the same time as Mark and watched Stan drive off before turning to face the driveway to the house.

She reached for Mark's hand.

He squeezed it and turned to her. 'You nervous?'

She nodded.

'Solita can be nasty with her tongue; just ignore it if you can.'

She nodded again.

They walked up to the front door and rang the bell. For a long time they heard nothing, then as Mark pressed the bell again, they heard footsteps, high heels on tile, approach the door. There was a pause, then the door was unlocked and opened.

A woman of similar age to Jane, with shoulder-length, brown hair draped around her sculptured, tanned face, looked Jane up and down. She pulled a face as if Jane was something distasteful before turning to Mark. It took only a moment before recognition came and she said, 'Adrian.'

'Solita,' Mark returned politely and turned to Jane. 'This is Jane.'

'She your whore?' Solita sneered, looking at Jane again.

Jane stiffened, but said nothing. She knew this was going to be hard for Mark and she didn't want to cause him more problems.

'Solita, watch your mouth,' Mark countered.

'Or what?' Solita challenged him, pushing her face towards him.

Mark shook his head and sighed. 'Let's not fight. Can we come in?'

Solita glared at him. 'You... you...'

For a moment Jane thought she was going to tell them to go away.

'You... fuc...' Solita stopped in mid-sentence, her eyes glancing past them to something in the road, then she begrudgingly stepped away from the door.

Mark took Jane's hand and they entered the house.

The front door opened into a small lounge area with an open-plan kitchen-diner off to the left. The decoration was light in colour and Jane could smell fresh paint. Two glass patio doors on the far wall opened out onto a small paved area with a green lawn ending at the exterior wall. The room felt cool from the air conditioning.

Solita pointed to the leather three-seater sofa in front of the wall-mounted fireplace and Jane and Mark sat down. Solita slid herself onto the two-seater sofa to their left, allowing her short cream dress to ride up, exposing most of her thighs.

Jane looked away to the room. The whole place was pristine and tidy. No children's toys, clothes or books lay around. In fact, the place didn't look lived-in.

She could feel Solita's eyes on her and turned her head

to stare back at her. Solita was holding a tight grin, a grin of someone holding a secret. Jane suddenly felt uncomfortable.

'Where are the children?' Mark asked.

Solita's eyes narrowed. 'Not here.'

Jane could feel Mark's anger in the tightness of his grip on her hand. 'I told you I wanted to see them. You promised they would be here.'

Solita smirked. 'You tell me what's so important and I'll go and get them. They're at a party.'

Jane didn't believe a word she said.

Mark sighed heavily. 'Ferrand won't stop hunting me and I've had enough of running, so I'm going to confront him.'

'What has that got to do with me?'

'Nothing, I just needed to see the children. I wanted to make sure they were safe.'

'Why?'

'Because I'm not going to give Ferrand what he wants and he may try to use them to force me to do it.'

Jane thought she saw a flicker of fear sweep across Solita's face. It was soon replaced with viciousness.

Solita sprung up like a wild cat ready to pounce. 'You fucking bastard. You've done it again, haven't you? You've endangered the lives of MY children for your own selfish ends!'

Mark lifted his hands in submission. 'Solita—'

'Don't you Solita me. You should have sold Ferrand your work in the first place.'

Mark stood up and faced her. 'I will never do that.'

'Then we're all going to suffer till Ferrand gets what he wants. Even your whore.' She turned to Jane and the glint in her eyes was wicked.

Mark stepped forward, making Solita turn her attention

to him. His voice was calm and controlled. 'I'll make you this deal. Let me see the children one more time, then take them somewhere safe. I'll resolve this with Ferrand and promise never to see…' he paused, swallowing deeply, '…the children again.'

Solita glared at him. 'Never?'

He nodded and croaked, 'Never.'

Solita grinned that secret grin again.

Jane stood up, annoyed at the obvious pleasure Solita was getting from Mark's pain. She moved to Mark's side.

Immediately, Solita's eyes were upon her, daggers of evil focusing on her face, searching for weaknesses.

'Solita!' Mark shouted. 'Do we have a deal?'

Slowly, Solita shifted her gaze to Mark and in a soft voice she whispered, 'Never again? You promise?'

Mark nodded.

A moment of silence followed, then Solita picked up her bag from the sofa. 'I'll go and fetch them, but I don't want *her* here.' She pointed purposely to Jane.

Mark began to protest, but Jane took his arm. 'It's okay; I'll wait outside when they come.'

Solita grinned again. 'I'll be fifteen minutes,' and walked to the door.

Mark caught her arm as she opened the door. Solita looked at him sharply. 'I'll be fifteen minutes, I said.'

Mark said nothing and let her go. The door closed behind her.

'You can't trust her, Mark,' Jane said quickly.

'What choice do I have?' he said wearily and returned to sit on the sofa.

It was the longest fifteen minutes Jane had ever experienced. They had hardly spoken and their eyes kept flicking up to the kitchen wall clock. As the last minute ticked over they heard a car pull onto the drive. They both jumped up. Mark was filled with excitement, but Jane felt apprehension. 'Shall I go out in the garden before they come in?' she asked in a whisper.

'NO,' Mark countered. 'I want you to meet them. I don't care what Solita says.' He took her hand and they walked to the front door.

Mark opened it.

A fist hit him in the face, sending him flat onto his back.

Jane stepped backwards, but not quickly enough. A tall, thickset man in jeans and sweater grabbed hold of her and forced her against the wall by the door. He held her firm, while a short, stocky man pushed past them and grabbed the front of Mark's shirt. He lifted him up and punched him brutally in the stomach.

Mark crumbled to the floor and lay gasping for breath as blood streamed down his face from his nose.

The tall man placed a hand on Jane's throat, pressing her against the wall while he swung the front door closed with the other.

Jane struggled to breathe, the pressure on her throat restricting her airway. She reached up and tried to force his hand away.

He leaned his face into hers. A cruel scar swept from his nose down his left cheek and his eyes were bloodshot. He grinned a set of yellow, stained teeth.

She could smell the greasiness of his brown hair over the whiff of his stale breath.

'Come on, darling.' He pulled her forward and gripped the back of her neck so tight with his other hand, it made Jane wince in pain. He pushed her towards the lounge.

Jane could feel her heart pounding in her head, its beating pulse deafening in her ears. Her stomach wanted to throw up and her legs wanted to collapse under her. She forced herself to stave off the faint that hovered inside and stay present.

The short, stocky man was kicking Mark repeatedly in the stomach.

'Eddie, the boss wants him alive.'

Eddie stopped kicking Mark and stood back. His black, curly hair fell over his eyes, but Jane knew he was looking at her. He grinned. 'What he say about her?'

Jane's throat suddenly choked up and her eyes widened as he turned towards her.

The tall man grabbed her long hair, yanking her head back so he could look down into her face.

Jane cried out and grasped his hand, trying to ease it from her hair.

A discoloured tongue rasped over her cheek and he laughed. 'Sure tastes good.' Then he slipped his right hand up under her blouse and into her bra.

Jane clawed at his face, ignoring the pain from her hair. She cut him under the right eye with her long fingernails.

'You bitch!' he yelled, withdrawing his hand from her breast to finger the blood slipping down his cheek. He stared at his fingers and a moment later backhanded her hard across the face.

Jane fell away from him to the floor, tearing her hair from his grasp. As soon as she was free, she scrambled for the front door.

He caught hold of one ankle and pulled her back towards him.

She kicked at his hand with her other foot, her fingers trying to find a grip on the tiles.

He grabbed both her feet and yanked her over onto her back.

The two men were on her; the tall one holding her down while Eddie sat astride her, his fingers fiddling with the button to undo her trousers.

She screamed and struggled, twisting and contorting her body in an attempt to free herself from their grip, but she knew she could not stop them.

Eddie had her trousers and pants down to her knees, when something happened. The grin on his face turned to a cringe and his hands went to his chest. Something lifted him off her and sent him flying backwards towards the glass doors at the far end of the room.

Her other attacker looked up, startled, before he grabbed his chest too and went flying over her in the direction of the two sofas.

It happened quickly but seemed also to be in slow motion. Jane raised herself up onto her elbows and saw Mark standing in the middle of the room. His hands curled like claws with pulsing red light coming out of his palms. His eyes were wide and staring manically from his blood-soaked face and his chest was heaving as if he was breathing heavily.

He focused on her and the wild expression softened, his hands relaxed and he looked around him, only now registering where he was and what had happened.

He rushed over, knelt down beside her and drew her into his arms. 'It's okay. You're safe.'

Jane gripped him tightly, her body shaking uncontrollably. She could see the men over his shoulder. Their chests had a circular burn mark on them as if they had been struck by lightning.

She closed her eyes. 'Thank you, thank you,' she

whispered, enjoying the warmth of Mark's body and his comforting, reassuring words.

She opened her eyes and gasped. Her throat seized closed, preventing her from uttering a sound. She dug her fingernails into his shirt.

Mark twisted round to see.

Eddie had risen to a crouched position, one hand to his chest, the other holding a flicked out knife. He rushed towards them, teeth bared in a vicious snarl.

Jane screamed.

Behind her, the front door burst open and she heard a gunshot.

Eddie fell to the floor, blood oozing from a small hole in his head. The tall man was on his feet drawing his gun from his waistband when the second gunshot came. His hand went to the bleeding hole in his stomach and his face seemed frozen in shock. Another bullet caught him between the eyes and he dropped to the floor.

Jane turned to look behind her. She knew it would be Stan.

He walked swiftly past her and Mark and checked each man, lingering briefly to finger the round burn marks on their chests.

Jane quickly pulled her pants and trousers up with shaking hands and Mark helped her to her feet.

'Sorry I was late,' Stan said, returning to them. He looked at Jane with concern. 'I didn't see them arrive.'

Jane just nodded her head; she couldn't speak. The room seemed to be stuffy and thick with the smell of blood. Her stomach was churning.

He turned to Mark. 'What happened to them?' He traced the image of a circle on his chest with his finger.

'I don't know,' Mark said, shaking his head.

Stan turned to Jane.

She diverted her gaze away to the floor, still struggling with the sickness inside. She didn't know how to explain it, she couldn't explain it, but obviously something had happened to Mark.

CHAPTER NINE

Stan hurried Jane and Mark to the car, then Jane saw him go back into the house. After a few minutes he came out with gloves on and was using a cloth to wipe down the door handle and bell button. Then he moved to the dark brown Chevrolet and opened the door of the driver's side. After a few minutes of searching inside he returned to their car.

'W... what were you searching for in the men's car?' Jane stammered, her body still reacting to the brutal attack on her.

Stan shrugged his shoulders. 'Thought it might give us a clue about who they were.'

'I know who they were,' Mark snuffled through the blood still pouring from his nose. 'They were Ferrand's men.'

Stan handed Mark some tissue paper. 'Clean yourself up. I'm going to put us some distance from this place.'

Mark put the tissue to his nose and muffled, 'Solita sold us out.'

'You don't know that,' Jane retorted. She didn't like standing up for his ex, but there was no proof she was involved. 'She might have been delayed. Oh my God! What if she returns with the children?'

Mark glanced back at her and she could see the same concern in his eyes.

'Well, from what you have told me,' Stan said, 'your ex is no fool and when she sees the strange Chevrolet in the drive, she'll drive on.'

Mark nodded his agreement and relaxed back into the front seat.

Jane let herself relax too and instantly began to tremble. She had nearly been raped, possibly killed. She could still feel the tall man's hands on her, still smell his sweat. She needed a shower; she needed to wash herself clean.

The trembling turned into shaking and she twisted her fingers round the edge of her blouse to stop it. This wasn't what she had expected. She hadn't prepared herself for being so involved with all the violence and the killing.

What the hell did you expect?' she scolded herself angrily. *Did you not realise the danger you were going to be in?*

Mark had tried to tell her, tried to get her to stay safe. Perhaps she should have listened to him and stayed with his parents. She sighed deeply. Maybe it was time for her to go home.

A sudden emptiness filled her stomach and she felt sick. In her mind she sensed a growing dread. Why was she feeling like this? Going home would save her, but it would also mean leaving Mark to his fate. A swirl of nausea hit her and she took deep breaths until it subsided.

She realised her body was reacting to her thoughts and couldn't understand how this urge to be with him was suffocating all rationale for her own safety. Could her fear of losing him and being alone be behind this? She wasn't sure. This dread was coming from deep within her and was stronger than anything she had felt before. It was overpowering her fear of staying here and she had no idea what it was.

★ ★ ★

Two hours later they were all sat in a motel room east of Holbrook on Interstate 40. Stan was examining the large bruise that was swelling Jane's right cheek. He handed her an icepack in a towel to put against it. His eyes flickered for a moment on the imprint of finger marks on her neck and he gently touched them.

'I'm really sorry about this, Jane,' he said softly.

She touched his hand as he pulled it away. 'It's okay; it's not your fault.'

A flicker of guilt seemed to catch on his face and he turned away to Mark who was sat on the bed. He examined Mark's damaged nose.

'It's broken…' He stopped and looked again. 'No, it's okay, you're lucky.' Stan sat down heavily in the chair next to the door. 'So what happened to those men? And don't tell me you don't know.'

Mark slowly shook his head. 'One minute I was on the floor choking in my own blood and next I heard Jane scream. I saw what they were doing to her and I got angry. So angry that…' – he paused as if trying to recall exactly how he had felt – '…this intense energy seemed to explode inside of me and the next thing I knew I was on my feet yanking the men off her.' He stared at his hands. 'But I didn't even touch them.'

Stan turned to Jane. 'What did you see?'

Jane told him and saw astonishment fall on Mark's face.

'What? How can this be?' He looked at his hands again.

Jane moved to sit with him on the bed and took hold of his hands. 'I don't know what's happened to you or how you did it, but you saved me and I'm glad you did.'

He smiled. 'Do you think it's some residual energy from bringing the power down in Africa to heal the crystals?'

'Could be, but how do we know it's all gone?'

'Well, if you get the feeling you are about to explode again, give us some warning, will you?' Stan said, smiling as he got up from the chair. He opened the cabinet by the TV, poured three glasses of whisky and handed them out. 'So where do we go from here?'

Mark reached for his rucksack and pulled out his laptop. 'We need to contact Solita. I'm going to email my father.' He connected to the Internet and his email pinged. He read it and looked up, surprised. 'It's from my dad. Solita has been in contact already. He says in her email she sounds pretty upset and is desperate for me to contact her. I have her mobile number.'

He picked up the room phone, but Stan caught his hand.

'Use this spare mobile instead. It's untraceable.' Stan unzipped his jacket pocket and handed him the phone.

Mark replaced the room's phone and dialled Solita's number on the mobile.

Jane heard the ringtone and seconds later it was answered.

'It's Adrian,' Mark said cautiously. He held the phone away from his ear as a barrage of abuse blasted down the line.

The abuse ebbed away and Jane could hear crying now.

'Solita, what's the matter?' Mark interrupted urgently.

The crying turned into sobs and Jane could hear the odd word that managed to squeeze out. 'Home… dead men… the children.'

Mark stiffened. 'What about the children? Solita, what about the children?'

Jane heard more sobs intermingled with muffled angry retorts. 'It's all your fucking fault…' Mark put his ear back to the phone and Jane heard no more.

'Solita, just tell me,' he yelled down the phone and got to his feet.

His face suddenly went pale.

He listened some more then said, 'Yes, I'll meet you. Where? No, somewhere public.'

Stan signalled to him and whispered, 'Flagstaff, diner on Route 66, the one with a toy train running around the walls.'

Mark nodded and relayed Stan's instructions. 'Tomorrow at 11.00am,' Mark confirmed and disconnected. He gave the mobile back to Stan and sat back on the bed, quietly staring at the floor.

'What is it?' Jane asked.

He looked at her and she noticed his eyes were watery.

'Ferrand has the children.'

★ ★ ★

Stan drove past the diner three times before 11.00am. Solita's car was parked in the car park and she was sitting in one of the booths facing the road. They pulled into the car park of the place next to the diner and Stan positioned the car so he could see them, but not be seen himself. It was also a good place to drive away from.

Jane adjusted the pink scarf around her neck to hide the bruising and got out of the car with Mark. She hadn't slept well, despite an hour long scrub in the shower and drinking a few large whiskys. The events of yesterday were still plaguing her mind and her body was still remembering its onslaught.

On top of that, she carried the guilt of not warning Solita. She had played the scene out in her mind over and over. Solita coming home with the children, the shock of two dead bodies in their lounge and then the children being brutally taken from their mother. She wondered whether Solita had been subjected to what she had at the hands of Ferrand's men, for even though she didn't know her, Jane suspected that Solita would not have let the children go easily.

Mark took her hand as they entered the diner and they walked straight to the booth where Solita was waiting. She turned to them as they reached her. Jane was surprised to see no bruises on her face or sore red eyes from her tears yesterday.

Solita glared at them both.

Jane slid into the booth first and Mark followed; a waitress came up and they ordered coffee.

When she had left, Solita snarled and jabbed a finger into Mark's chest. 'This is your fault. You led them to us.'

Jane felt more guilt sweep over her, despite Stan's assurance that there had been no way Ferrand's men had tracked them.

'Tell me what happened,' Mark said quietly.

Solita sat back and waited until the waitress had placed the coffee on the table and moved out of earshot before she spoke. 'I came home and found two dead men on the floor,' she whispered bitterly.

'What about the children?' Mark said, shifting anxiously in his seat.

'What do you think? They were traumatised. All that blood and gore.'

Mark stiffened.

'They wouldn't stop crying,' Solita said earnestly, 'you made them cry.' She paused as if waiting for a reply. 'They think you're a murderer.'

Jane saw Mark flush and shake his head. 'I didn't want this,' he whispered, lowering his head.

Jane caught a look of delight on Solita's face and she suddenly thought something was wrong.

'I didn't kill them,' Mark said firmly.

Solita stared at him. 'Who did, then?' She glanced at Jane. 'Not your whore, then.'

Mark looked up sharply. 'Stop calling her that!' he whispered hoarsely. He composed himself before adding, 'We have a friend…'

Jane pinched his leg hard and he immediately shut up.

Solita swallowed and looked around. 'Where is he?'

Mark ignored her question. 'How did Ferrand get the children? Are they all right?'

Solita laughed at him. 'All right!' she yelled. 'You think they're all right after this?'

Mark cleared his throat with a cough. 'I know, but Ferrand didn't hurt them, did he?'

Solita softened her voice. 'We had just arrived home when more of his men pulled into the drive. They grabbed the children and told me I had forty-eight hours to deliver you or they will kill…' Her voice suddenly broke off, '… the children.' Solita opened her handbag and pulled out a tissue. She dabbed her eyes. 'You have to give yourself up, Adrian. You have to, for the children.' She began to sob into the tissue.

Mark gently took Solita's hand and squeezed it. 'He won't harm them. Tell Ferrand he can have me in exchange for the children.'

'When?' Solita said, almost too gleefully.

'Tomorrow. I'll ring you with a time and place.'

Solita suddenly became anxious. 'No! Today. You can't make the children suffer another day.'

Mark took a deep breath and sighed.

Jane knew he was fighting with Stan's instructions to delay so Stan would have time to prepare.

'Adrian, please! Don't let them suffer,' Solita cried, sniffing back more sobs.

Mark finally gave in. 'Okay, this afternoon. I'll call you with a place and time.'

Solita smiled slyly, but Jane caught sight of it.

Mark got up to go, but Jane pulled him down and when he looked at her, she raised her eyebrows. He had blown Stan's instructions once already and was about to blow them again. She saw understanding show on his face.

'I'll call you, Solita, in about an hour.' He reached over the table and took the bill slip for her coffee. 'I'll get this, so you can go.'

The disappointment on Solita's face was clear. She stood up sharply and without another word she left the diner.

Jane watched her strut to her car, her high heels tapping across the tarmac, her short, flowered, cotton dress shifting upwards with each swing of her hips.

Solita paused as she opened the car door and looked around the car park at all the empty cars. She finally got into her car and drove off in the direction of Flagstaff.

Mark settled the bills and they left the diner. Instead of returning the way they came, they walked through the car park to the far end and then along the road until they entered another car park to a group of shops. Within minutes, Stan pulled in and picked them up. Back at the motel, it was clear Stan wasn't happy with Mark's change of plan.

'What were you thinking?' Stan scolded.

'I was thinking of my children,' Mark countered.

Stan sat down and pondered. 'You know there's a big risk he won't exchange the children.'

Mark nodded. 'How can we ensure that he does?'

Stan raised his hands in a gesture that said, "How do

I know?" He looked at the floor for a moment as if some thought had come to him and then got up. 'Call your ex. Tell her that Ferrand must be the one to make the swap. You won't deal with his men.' Mark nodded and Stan continued, 'You know what Ferrand looks like?' Mark nodded again.

'What are you going to do?' Jane asked, worried about where this was going.

'I'm going to cover Mark at the drop-off and when the exchange occurs, I'll kill Ferrand.'

Jane went to speak, but closed her mouth. She didn't want anyone else to get hurt, yet she knew Stan's solution would resolve the problem once and for all. But could she be party to murder?

'Do you have to kill him?' she whispered. 'Can't you not just scare him off?'

Stan swirled round to her and the look on his face made her sit back. 'You still don't get it,' he said angrily. 'He doesn't care about you, or Mark, or the children. He has no morals, and it won't bother him one bit to let his men rape or torture you and the children.'

Jane shuddered.

'He'll use you to get what he wants and when he's finished, he'll kill you and he'll make Mark watch just for the fun of it, before killing him too.' Stan took a step towards her and his tone was as cold as steel. 'You should have stayed at home.'

Jane couldn't stop the tears. They burst from her in a torrent, making her whole body shake. Mark was at her side in a second. His arms around her. Jane sobbed out her emotions. She didn't know what else to do. She was in something that was out of her depth with a tidal wave about to overwhelm her. She desperately wanted to run away as fast as she could, but the deep, ingrained urge to stay, scared her.

Stan squatted down in front of her and took her hands. 'Sorry, Jane. I didn't mean to upset you.' He took a deep breath. 'You are a brave woman and you've gone through some stuff, but maybe it's time you stepped back from the frontline.'

Jane sniffed back more tears and was about to reject his idea when he squeezed her hands and said, 'Mark is safe with me; don't worry.'

It was as if a huge stone of burden had been removed from her back. She trusted him and he had given her an opportunity to escape the situation she found herself in. Slowly, she nodded and saw a sense of relief fall over both men. Mark gave her a hug and kissed her head while Stan just patted her hands.

He stood up and grabbed a map from his bag, which he set upon the table. Jane wiped away her tears and moved over with Mark to see.

'We need an open space but with cover,' Stan said, then his finger landed on a place called Sedona. 'When you call your ex, tell her Ferrand needs to meet you at Cathedral Rock car park at 4.30pm. Ask her to pick you up in Sedona, outside Safeway at 4.00pm.'

Jane looked at him. 'Why does Solita have to pick Mark up?'

Stan stared at her incredulously. 'I need time to set up and I can't be in two places at the same time, can I?'

'Well, I could drive Mark in,' she countered, a little annoyed at his sarcasm.

Stan shook his head. 'You will stay here. Less for me to worry about. Anyway, Solita will get the children and drive away before Mark gives himself to Ferrand.'

'So how will you know who Ferrand is?'

'Mark will give me a sign. I expect Ferrand will have some men with him.'

'What sort of sign?' Mark asked.

Stan thought for a moment. 'Have your hands in your pockets when they arrive. If Ferrand is with them, take your hands out. Then when the children are freed, walk directly to Ferrand.'

'What if Ferrand isn't there?' Jane cut in quickly.

Stan smiled. 'Then I'll lay down some cover fire for Mark and Solita to escape.'

Jane sighed; it all sounded smooth and organised, so why was her stomach twitching so badly?

Stan moved to the door. 'I need to get ready.' He left the room.

Mark picked up the phone and made the call to Solita.

A short while later Stan was knocking on the room door. He was dressed in pale, sandy-coloured camouflage trousers and shirt and had two large black canvas bags. Mark helped him carry them to the car.

Jane didn't ask what was in the bags. Part of her already knew. She had no idea how Stan managed to get hold of his weapons, but he did seem to know a lot of people in many places.

She waited by the door until they'd finished packing.

Mark returned and took her into his arms. He kissed her hard and full.

She could feel his need for her as his body pressed against hers, and she gripped him tight, afraid to let go, fearful she may never see him again. Her heart was telling her she should go with him, should be by his side, yet her head was justifying why she needed to stay.

He pulled away and was about to go when she grabbed

him again, curling her arms around his body. 'I don't want you to go,' she whispered fiercely, feeling her emotions rushing through her body, ready to explode.

He kissed her on her head and pulled himself out of her grip.

'It'll be okay. I'll see you later.'

Jane nodded and her body shuddered.

Stan came up and slapped Mark hard on the left shoulder. 'Right, time to go,' he said jovially.

'Jesus, Stan!' Mark exclaimed, rubbing his shoulder. 'That hurt.'

'Oh, sorry; just wanted to check you were awake. Let's go.'

Jane frowned and eyed Stan with puzzlement. *What is up with him? Why is he excited and almost happy?* The momentary distraction passed and Stan and Mark left.

Jane watched both men get into the car.

The car started and Stan drove it to the car park exit.

A huge urge rushed through her body. She wanted to call them back, to scream for them to stop! She gripped the door frame hard, forcing herself to continue to watch as the car slipped out of sight. For a moment, she stared at the empty space where the car had been and from somewhere inside, a cold finger of fear began to make itself known. Jane forced herself to close the door and sit on the bed. It would be hours before they returned, if they returned. A sob caught in her throat and tears crept into her eyes. She stared at the wall and her mind screamed, *This is a big mistake!*

CHAPTER TEN

Half an hour after Mark and Stan had left, the room phone rang, stirring Jane from her excessive pacing. She grabbed it. 'Yes?' she said, her voice strained.

'Oh, it's you,' Solita's bitter tone came back. 'Put Adrian on.'

'He's gone. What do you want?' Jane could feel her anger rising.

'Fuck!'

Jane became uneasy. 'Why have you called?' She heard frantic, muffled whispering, but couldn't distinguish what was being said. Jane hardened her voice to disguise the panic rising in her. 'What is it you want?'

'Hmm, I forgot what time I had to pick him up.'

Jane knew Solita was lying; her whole body felt Solita's lie, but what could she do? Anger returned. 'FOUR PM! OUTSIDE SAFEWAY!'

The phone went dead.

'Bitch!' Jane shouted at the phone as she put it down.

She sat on the edge of the bed for a moment to allow her anger to subside, her hand resting on the receiver. Her mind was trying to tell her something, something important, but she couldn't decipher what it was. There was something wrong about that call, but what was it? She began to pace the room again, going over every word of the conversation. Her stomach was cringing and felt heavy; her body was telling her this was important, but her mind couldn't grasp the meaning.

After fretting for ten minutes, Jane went to the bathroom and relieved herself. She then splashed her face with cool water, but the distraction wasn't working; she couldn't subdue the panic building up inside her. It sloshed about in her stomach, making her feel sick.

She walked back into the room and focused on the phone. 'What is it?' she pleaded to herself, her voice abnormally loud in the silence.

A car pulled up outside.

Are they back so soon? She glanced at the clock. It showed 3.30pm. Her eyes shifted to the phone. *Why did Solita ring? How did she know what number to call?* Jane quickly turned to the door, her breath catching in her throat as she realised the door was unlocked and the person or people approaching from the car couldn't be Stan or Mark.

She sprang forward, grabbing for the lock as the door forced open against her. She twisted back into the room, running for the bathroom, but the man caught hold of her before she could get inside and lock the door. He forced her right arm up behind her back as he pushed her against the back wall of the room. Jane could feel the pressure of his body against her back as his head came close to hers. His breath was warm on her ear as he said, 'No screaming; otherwise, I'll have to hurt you.'

Jane stiffened her body and squeezed her eyes closed, waiting for the onslaught of his hands on her body, but none came; instead, he released her arm and roughly turned her to face him. She opened her eyes, fear making her tremble as he stared down into her face.

He wasn't like the other men Ferrand employed; he was clean-shaven and smartly dressed. He looked to be in his forties, maybe slightly older as his short, brown hair was greying at the edges. A big man, not fat, whose chest filled his shirt and suit jacket.

He was frowning, but immediately checked himself and secured a hand tightly around her upper right arm.

They walked to the door where a younger man was leaning against the frame. A cigarette hung from his lower lip and he was absently scratching one of the many spots on his face. He straightened his lanky body and pulled the cigarette from his mouth. 'Come on, girl, you and me in the back.'

Jane froze, causing the man holding her to walk into her.

'You're driving,' he grunted to the younger man and pushed Jane forward.

'But I think she likes me,' the young man said, moving towards her.

Jane stepped back.

The man holding her promptly moved her aside and grabbed the front of the young man's shirt. 'I said drive!'

The young man scowled at him and pulled away. 'Later then,' he sneered.

Jane took a deep breath and her body visibly relaxed. She felt the hand on her arm tighten a little and then she was pushed out of the door and into the car.

During the journey no one spoke. Jane sat very still on the back seat, her hands gripped together on her lap. She knew the man next to her was capable of countering any move she made to escape, so she resigned herself to being there and tried to distract her mind about what lay ahead by looking out of the window.

The landscape was barren and beautiful. Semi-desert, with red and grey ground intermingling and contrasting wonderfully when the patches of green grazing fields met it. She would have appreciated it more had her mind not kept on flashing up questions about the situation she was in. What would happen now that Ferrand had her? How could Stan cover that? Was Stan right about what Ferrand would do once Mark gave him what he wanted? Would they all die?

She shivered involuntarily, desperate to cling to some hope all would turn out okay, but her rational mind could not see that happening. Her situation was beyond help and it brought her a burden of sadness. She gave a big sigh.

She felt a touch on her arm and turned to look at the man next to her. A tear slipped down her cheek as her heavy emotion released silently. There was something in his eyes, a moment of connection and a look of reassurance.

He looked away.

She returned to the view out of the window. In her mind she sent out a wish for help and in the deep recesses of her helplessness a spark of light began to develop. *Maybe there could be some hope to have after all.*

As they travelled, the scenery changed to a canyon of cliffs and trees with a river running alongside the road. The cliffs were red and a sign on the road said "Sedona". It wasn't long before the car pulled off the main road and down a small, rough track. The sun was low in the sky as they pulled into a nearly deserted car park.

Jane saw Mark standing stiffly beside Solita's Chevrolet and Solita was next to him in her cream, flowery dress, absently kicking the dirt with her calf-length brown boots. Opposite them was a black Dodge Ram with two men standing in front of it. They looked like cowboys in their jeans and checked shirts.

Jane noticed Mark had his hands in his trouser pockets.

Her car drew up next to the Dodge Ram and when it stopped, the man next to her got out and pulled her after him.

Jane saw the shock on Mark's face and his eyes widen with worry at the sight of her.

She was walked up to the two men in front of the Dodge Ram.

'Been waiting for yer, Mac,' one said.

The man holding her growled at him, making the cowboy back away. Mac said in a loud voice, 'Adrian, don't make me hurt your woman. Walk slowly over here.'

Jane saw Mark hesitate before standing his ground. 'My children, where are my children?'

Solita started to laugh; she swung round to face him, her face full of joy. 'You sap. You believed me.'

'Ferrand... he hasn't the children?' Mark mumbled.

Solita laughed again. 'Yeah, but him and me. You know.' She joined two fingers together.

Mark just stared at her.

Jane felt Mac tighten his grip on her arm. He looked around and up, then bent his head close to hers. 'We know he has someone watching his back,' he whispered. 'Where is he?'

Jane shook her head. 'I don't know.'

Mac suddenly pulled her close to him and from a pocket in his jacket he drew a gun, which he pressed hard against her temple. 'Adrian,' he shouted, louder than was needed. 'I will shoot your woman if you don't come with us and...' He paused, looking at specific spots high up, 'I will shoot her if your man opens fire on us.'

Jane saw Mark's shoulders sag and when he looked across at her, she saw despair on his face. With his hands still in his pockets, he walked slowly towards them.

Solita giggled with pleasure, clapping her hands like a delighted child.

Jane wanted to hit her.

When Mark reached them, the two cowboys grabbed him and forced him into the Ram. At the same time, Mac backed Jane and himself to their car's rear door and got in, pulling Jane in after him. Solita got into her Chevrolet and led the procession of cars out of the car park. Once on the road, they picked up speed.

Jane glanced back at the dust cloud they left behind and wondered what, if anything, Stan could do for them now.

CHAPTER ELEVEN

They drove for some time until Jane saw a large water globe on a tall pillar with the name Tuba City on it. They turned left at the junction and followed the road for what seemed like miles before turning off onto a dirt road, which took them across the desert and towards some mountains. At the base of the mountains, the track swung round to the left and carried on until Jane saw a fenced-off piece of land.

Solita got out and opened the gate. She waited until all the cars had driven through before she drove her car forward and closed the gate behind it.

The track continued between the mountains until Jane saw a one-level sandy-coloured house with a glass front.

The cars stopped in front of the double doors and Mac took hold of Jane's arm as they got out of the car. She stood quietly next to him and watched as Mark was unnecessarily manhandled out of the Ram by the two cowboys. He looked despondent and weary.

Solita swaggered past and smiled a sly, satisfied smile at Jane.

Jane surged forward, unable to contain her anger any longer. She wanted to smash that smile off Solita's face.

Mac's tight grip brought her to an abrupt halt and he pulled her back.

Jane twisted round and glared at him.

He just shook his head.

She let the force of anger dissipate with a big huff and

watched Solita continue to strut towards the entrance. *God, she hated that woman.*

Mac pulled her closer to him as they all followed Solita through the glass front doors into a marble-floored hallway. Solita opened the door to a larger room to the right and they walked in past her.

The marbled floor from the hallway continued into the room. Jane noticed the room was sparsely furnished for its size. There were two smoky-glass windows overlooking a manicured lawn and flowered garden, which seemed unnatural and not in keeping with the desert and mountain beyond it. A large dining-room table and chairs were positioned to one side of the windows so as not to obstruct the view from the fireplace that was on the rear wall. A light-tanned leather sofa sat at an angle to the fire so as to allow a view of both the fire and the garden. In front of it there was a coffee table with a large weaved rug beneath it.

Jane's attention shifted to the far corner of the rear wall, which dipped away from sight into an alcove. It was strangely dark and the outline of the back of a black armchair was just visible.

Solita pushed past, shoving Jane hard on the shoulder.

Jane swung round to confront her, but Mac caught hold of her other arm and held her back.

Solita stepped away out of her reach and smirked, before moving to the windows.

Jane took a long deep breath to calm her emotions and Mac eased his hold on her.

She looked for Mark and saw him standing nearby between the two cowboys. He looked devastated, fearful even, and Jane's anger quickly disappeared. She wanted to hold him, tell him it would be all right, but how could she do that when she didn't believe it herself?

A spotty face blocked her vision of Mark. The watery, glazed eyes flickered from her face to her body and he gave her a lecherous grin.

She quickly looked away, shuddering.

A man's deep, throaty voice echoed into the room. 'You men, except Mac, can go.'

The spotty man looked disappointed for a moment, but didn't argue and left with the others. When the door was closed, a grey-haired man, wearing a white shirt and khaki trousers, moved out of the shadows of the alcove and into the room.

As he drew nearer to the light, Jane's eyes were drawn to the pure white, unmarked shoes, then to the bright red neckerchief, before finally focusing on the tanned and wrinkled face of Ferrand.

He walked to the windows and glanced out into the garden for what seemed like a long time. The room was silent and everyone was watching him. He finally turned and looked at Mac. He said nothing.

Mac seemed to know the question for he said, 'No sign, sir; but he was there.'

Ferrand nodded.

Solita seemed unable to contain her delight any longer. She rushed up to Ferrand and smoothed her hand over his chest. 'You have him now. Remember our agreement. I don't care what you do to him, just give me my money and me and the children will be off.'

Jane saw what Solita did not: a flash of anger sweep across Ferrand's face.

He suddenly caught hold of her hand and twisted it cruelly. Solita yelped and tried to release herself, but Ferrand twisted it more, sending Solita to her knees. He bore down on her, his face in a vicious snarl. 'You can have your money, but not the children.' He threw her hand away from him.

Solita cradled it to her chest. 'You said I could have them!' she screamed.

Ferrand turned away from her. 'NO! They stay!' He took a deep breath as if controlling his anger, then his voice softened slightly. 'I may have need to hurt them.'

Solita's eyes narrowed; her lips pulled back against her white teeth in a face etched with fury.

She inched herself off her knees to a crouched position and slipped her right hand down her leg to something in her calf boot.

She sprung at him, a dagger in her hand.

She was quick, but Ferrand was faster. He swung round, grabbed her dagger hand and bent it inwards towards her body. Then with the full force of his whole body, he pushed the dagger up into her chest.

Solita staggered back, blood staining the front of her flowered dress, her face frozen in shock and disbelief. She looked down at the knife and fell to the floor.

Mark quickly rushed over to her. He knelt down and Solita gripped his shirt collar with a bloodied hand. Her mouth moved, her lips forming whispered words no one could hear. A moment later her hand dropped to the floor and she moved no more.

Mark slowly stood up. 'W… Why?' he stammered.

Ferrand came up beside him and put a hand on his shoulder. He looked down at Solita's body as if looking at something vaguely interesting. 'Why?' he said ponderingly. 'Well, Adrian, you see, I don't need her anymore.'

Mark looked at him. 'So if you don't need the children either, will you kill them too?'

Ferrand raised an eyebrow. 'Hmm, maybe.'

Mark's eyes widened with alarm. 'Look, I'll give you what you want if you will let the children go with Jane, unharmed.'

Ferrand laughed and patted Mark on the shoulder.

'Ah, you expect me to trust you? There, you see, is where we differ.' Ferrand walked over to Jane. 'I am wondering how long you will give me what I want without any leverage.' He caught Jane under the chin with his finger. 'I could let the children go, and work on this lovely lady for a bit, but I think you may still hold back.'

Jane held her body rigid, her eyes drawn to his face. Ferrand's tone was friendly, his words deadly, but it was the intensity of his stare that scared her more than anything.

He moved back to Mark and put his arm around Mark's shoulders like a friend would. 'But, I will have even greater leverage if I have your children too. Perhaps they could watch me dissect their mother and if you still didn't fully cooperate, I would have you watch while I dissected each of them in turn, while keeping them alive.'

Mark shook his head violently.

Ferrand laughed. 'So you see, Adrian, it will be your children and your woman that will ensure I get what I want.' He turned away and spoke to Mac. 'Take them away.'

Mac moved towards the door, but Jane's body was shaking so badly she struggled to move. Her legs wobbled and she stumbled against him. He slipped his arm around her to give her support.

She tried to focus on the door they were headed for, but her mind would not let go of what she had just seen and heard. Ferrand was a dangerous man. No, he was more than that; he was a monster. She dimly heard Mark's voice behind her.

'I want to see my children.'

Mac stopped and Ferrand nodded to him. 'This way,' Mac said and they all left the room.

Outside, the two cowboys moved to either side of Mark, but Jane knew it was unnecessary, for Mark wasn't going to resist or try to escape. The slump of his head and the shuffle of his feet on the floor told her he was beaten.

Mac took them to a room at the back of the house. He unlocked the door and they all entered.

Mark's two children were playing with toy cars on a mat. The boy was in brown trousers and a white t-shirt and his sister was dressed in soft, patterned leggings and a pretty pink blouse. They looked up and there was puzzlement on the boy's face. Jane waited by the door with Mac and watched.

Mark moved into the room and knelt down. 'Hiya, Jamie,' he said softly.

The boy looked at him as if trying to figure out any recognisable features on Mark's face.

Mark smiled at him.

The boy suddenly yelled, 'Daddy,' and rushed forward. He stopped just before Mark's open arms, hesitating, then flung himself into Mark's body.

Mark held his son tightly, his face buried into the boy's shoulder. Finally, he looked up and over to Jane.

She could see his eyes were watery, his emotions on the verge of spilling out.

Jane could feel tears in her eyes too. She knew how it felt to lose someone you love, but she could only imagine how it must feel to love your children and not be able to see or be with them.

Jamie pulled back and looked at Mark's face. 'What's the matter, Daddy?'

Mark brushed a hand over his eyes. 'Nothing, I'm just so happy to see you.'

Jamie put his hands on each side of Mark's face and looked into his eyes. 'And I'm happy to see you too. Are we going home soon?' He searched his dad's face and frowned, somehow registering Mark's anguish.

Jane noticed that Mark's daughter was still standing by the toys. She was fidgeting from one foot to the other, waiting with uncertainty as to what she should do next.

Mark pulled Jamie into his right side and stretched out his left hand to her, encouraging her to come forward. She frowned, not recognising who he was and unsure if she should move.

Jamie waved to her to come. 'It's Daddy, come on.'

She still didn't move. Her eyes fixed on Jane for a moment, then diverted to Mac and back to Jamie. Jane knew she was searching for her mother.

Jamie moved from Mark's embrace and went to her. He grabbed her arm. 'Sophie, it's Daddy,' he said again and yanked her forward.

Sophie fixed her feet firmly in place and shook her head.

Jamie seemed confused, then grabbed her round the chest and lifted her off the ground to carry her over.

Sophie screamed and kicked out, twisting herself out of Jamie's grasp. She fled to the farthest wall and slid to the floor, under the boarded-up window, crying.

Jamie was about to go after her when Mark stopped him. 'No, Jamie, let her be.'

Jamie turned to him and Jane could see the boy was upset.

'It's okay,' Mark said gently, beckoning Jamie to come back to him. Jamie returned and Mark put his arm around his son. 'Sophie needs some time…' He paused as if choked up, '… To get to know me.'

Jamie put his arms around Mark's neck, but suddenly pulled back. 'Daddy, you're bleeding.'

Mark pushed his bloodied collar under so it was out of sight. 'It was a nose bleed,' he said softly and pointed to his bruised, swollen nose.

Jamie accepted his explanation without question and repeated, 'Can we go home now?'

Mark shook his head. 'I have to do something first, then we can go. Until then, I need you to look after your sister. Can you do that?'

Jamie turned to look at Sophie who was quietly watching them. 'Yes,' he said and moved to go to her.

Mark gently pulled him back and kissed the top of his head before saying, 'You see that lady at the door?' Jamie turned to look at Jane. 'Her name is Jane.' Mark paused as if uncertain he should proceed. He looked over to her.

Jane nodded; she knew what was coming next.

'She's a very nice lady and she'll look after you and your sister until I finish what I have to do.'

Jamie stared at Jane for a moment before turning back to Mark. 'Where's Mummy?'

Mark swallowed before speaking. 'She's had to go away,' he lied, 'but Jane and I will take care of you and Sophie.'

'Okay,' Jamie said matter-of-factly and moved to his sister. He sat down beside her and offered her a soft toy rabbit.

Mark got up quickly and moved to join Jane.

She noticed he was struggling to restrain his emotions. She took his hand and squeezed it.

He gave her a weak smile and turned to Mac. 'I want Jane to look after them. They… they need someone to be here.'

Mac didn't say anything. He glanced across to the two children and then nodded.

'Thank you,' Mark said, relieved; then he turned to Jane and gave her a peck on the cheek. 'Will you be okay with the children?'

Jane gently touched his face and kissed him on the lips. She could feel the turmoil raging inside of him. She drew back and smiled. 'Yes and don't worry, we'll be just fine.'

Mac opened the door and he and Mark left.

Jane turned her back to the door and looked at the children huddled against the wall. Jamie was trying to get Sophie to play with him, without much luck.

She took a deep breath and thought, *What the hell do I do here?* Her experience with children was zero; there had been no opportunity for any interaction at all. Her life had been filled with work, meetings and the odd social occasion; she had no idea of what to say or do.

She moved to the centre of the room and sat on the mat where a selection of toys was spread out. A deep sigh slipped from her lips and seemed to rest heavily on her shoulders. The situation looked bleak. She didn't think they would survive even if Mark gave Ferrand what he wanted. The poor children; they had no idea what they were involved in.

She looked at the toys and thought, *What can I do for these kids?*

A gentle touch on her shoulder stirred her from her thoughts and she looked up. Jamie was stood in front of her; his blue eyes surveyed her face and she saw him frown at the bruising on her left cheek and throat.

Jane touched her cheek and said, 'I had an accident.'

He hesitated before speaking. 'Don't be sad, Daddy will be back soon.'

111

Jane nodded. She hoped so, but her mind was saying it was all so hopeless.

Jamie handed her a book. 'Will you read to us?'

Jane took it, read the title "Daisy Dog: My Daddy comes home" and smiled at the picture on the front; a cartoon father dog cuddling his two children. It was so appropriate. Just as she was opening the front cover, Sophie came and stood by her side, clutching the toy rabbit. 'You want to hear the story too?' Jane asked.

Sophie stuck her thumb in her mouth and nodded, then she ducked under Jane's arm and snuggled down onto her lap.

Jamie hesitated about doing the same; instead, he sat down next to her on the mat. Jane opened the book and began to read.

CHAPTER TWELVE

It was early evening and Jane was sitting next to the two cot beds where Sophie and Jamie were sleeping, watching the slow deep rhythm of their breathing. She noticed that their soft, smooth faces seemed content and peaceful. Sophie was snuggled into her toy rabbit, her thumb in her mouth and Jamie was laid on his back with his arms flung out above his head. Under their closed eyelids there were random movements of their eyes and she knew they were dreaming. She hoped their dreams were of nice things.

She heard the soft click of the door lock and turned to see Mac in the doorway. He motioned her to come with him. Silently, she got up from the cushion on the floor and stepped quietly around the toys to where Mac was waiting. As she got to him, she noticed he was watching the children and for a moment she thought she saw a flicker of softness in his face.

She slipped out of the room and waited while Mac relocked it. He indicated for her to move to the large room where she and Mark had seen Ferrand. She tensed with sudden fear, remembering the events earlier, her thoughts returning to Ferrand's threat and promise to cause her suffering should Mark not cooperate.

Mac opened the door and they went inside.

Ferrand was sitting at the dining table by the front windows. There was an assortment of food laid out and Mac drew out a chair for her at the table. Jane sat down, her eyes fixed on Ferrand.

He got up, picked up a jug of water and poured some into a glass, which he placed on the table in front of her.

Jane took the glass, only now realising that she had not had a drink all day. She finished it in seconds.

'Jane. It is all right to call you Jane?' Ferrand asked, almost friendly, as he refilled her glass. He continued without waiting for her reply. 'I'm going to need your help.'

Jane didn't think for one minute that Ferrand needed any help from her. She watched him put the jug down and turn to her.

'You see, I want Adrian to give me the crystal and the power behind it, but …' He paused for effect. 'I think that perhaps Adrian may try to deceive me.'

Jane didn't say anything; she just stared at him, but her heart was starting to pound.

Ferrand's voice softened and there was just a hint of concern in his tone. 'I don't want to hurt you or the children, believe me. And it will give me no pleasure to make you suffer.'

Jane looked into his eyes and saw the lie.

He smiled and turned away, misdirecting her for a moment before lunging back and grabbing her right wrist. He twisted it, squeezing the flesh against the bone.

Jane gasped and tried to pull away.

He tightened his grip and twisted it some more.

The pain was so intense Jane tried to stand up.

Mac's firm hands rested on her shoulders, pushing her back down.

Tears flooded into her eyes, but Jane refused to yell, keeping her mouth tightly shut. She looked defiantly at Ferrand and saw the gleam of pleasure on his face.

She suddenly became afraid.

His grip lessened and he turned her hand so it lay flat, palm down, on the table. He reached across to the centre of the table and picked up a lighted candle.

Jane's breathing quickened as she realised what he intended to do. Her body stiffened and she pushed herself back into the chair.

Ferrand placed the candle by her hand and lifted her wrist up, forcing her curled fingers out with his other hand so she could not make a fist.

'NO!' Jane shouted, moving her other hand in to stop him, but Mac caught hold of it and pulled it back to her shoulder. She watched in a blinking haze as Ferrand moved her palm over the candle flame. At first, there was no sensation, then he forced it lower and she felt heat followed by a burning of her flesh. She screamed.

It was the signal Ferrand was waiting for. He immediately let go of her.

Jane drew her burnt hand to her chest, cradling it as tears slipped down her cheeks. The centre of her palm was red and blistered.

Mac handed her a wet cloth and Jane wrapped it over the wound.

Ferrand walked round the back of her chair. 'Like I said, Jane, I don't want you or the children to suffer, but this is just a fraction of what I will do to you and them if I don't get Adrian's full cooperation. You understand?'

Jane nodded.

'You must convince him to give me what I want.'

Jane wiped away the tears. The thought of him doing this to the children was unbearable. She could not allow this to happen.

Ferrand nodded to Mac who left the room.

Jane could feel Ferrand's eyes on her as he returned to the chair at the head of the table. A moment later the door opened and Mac returned with Mark.

'Ah, Adrian, come and join us,' Ferrand said pleasantly.

Jane looked up and saw Mark staring at her.

Concern flashed across his face when he saw the cloth on her hand. He came straight to her, his eyes flickering from her face to her cradled hand. Before he could touch her, Mac pushed him into the chair next to hers.

'What's happened?' he whispered, reaching for her hand.

Jane shook her head and her eyes welled up with tears. She looked away and focused on the candle.

'The same thing that will happen to your children, if you don't cooperate,' Ferrand said bluntly.

Mark took Jane's hand and eased the cloth away. His face angered and he shot to his feet.

Mac was ready for him and pushed him back down.

'I told you I would do what you wanted,' Mark yelled in frustration.

'Ah, yes, but for how long?'

Jane saw Mark look away guiltily and she knew he had obviously thought about doing something to stop or delay Ferrand. He glanced across to her and she saw him slowly shake his head. He was defeated and it sounded in his voice. 'I will do whatever you want me to do.'

Jane saw Ferrand's smug smile. He had vanquished his enemy, suppressed any defiance or resistance. 'You had a crystal in Africa, a special one you used at my mine. It was bigger than the one you first created.'

Mark looked at him in surprise. 'How…' He paused as if trying to figure it out before he finally said, 'How do you know this?'

'Solita was very thorough in her betrayal of you. She described what she saw when she sent me a photo of it with a copy she made of your notes. But the information was incomplete, wasn't it?' Ferrand paused as if waiting for Mark to reply, but he didn't. 'At my mine in Africa the experiment with the crystal didn't work, but then you turned up and the surveillance cameras showed you had a different crystal. It looked more powerful.'

Mark's body slumped deeper into his chair and he heaved a big sigh.

Jane could feel his despair and sadness. He had been tricked by the person he had loved. Her heart went out to him. Then anger began to ferment. All this had come about because Solita had wanted money and to be rid of him as a father to her children. The cruelty of the woman was unbelievable. The anger suddenly subsided as the memory of Solita's body lying on Ferrand's floor, returned. In the end, all Solita got was her own betrayal and ultimately her death. Poetic justice, some would say, but Jane couldn't find anything to be happy about. Her attention returned to Ferrand, who was speaking.

'I want you to create another crystal like the one in Africa, but it has to fit this artefact.' He got up and moved to the dark alcove. From out of the corner, he brought out something that was covered in a silk-like cloth. He pulled off the cover and revealed a metallic structure supported on a tripod. The structure was shaped like two hollow pyramids, one upright and the other upside down, with their bases touching each other at the points where the tripod's legs were attached to it.

At the centre, where the bases came together, was a shape Jane remembered seeing in Greece and again in Glastonbury. It was the Vesica Piscis, two overlapping cycles creating an oval centre. In the oval centre there seemed to be metal clips to hold something. *The crystal*, she thought.

Ferrand's face beamed with delight as he gently touched it, almost caressing it. 'The crystal will sit inside and extend above and below into the pyramids,' he said to no one in particular. 'It will bring heaven and earth together and give me the power of one.'

Something in Jane seemed to resonate with his last words. She could see that Mark was experiencing the same thing, but the expression on his face was a mix of amazement and absolute terror.

'Wh… where did you get it?' Mark said, his hands rubbing on his trousers as if they were sweaty.

Ferrand turned to him as if pleased to be asked. 'It came from a dig in Barbados. An underwater cavern from deep in the earth.' He fingered the pyramid edges. 'It is a remnant of a civilisation long ago, a civilisation that worked with crystals and was able to harness the life force of the universe and the world we live in.'

'Atlantis,' Mark whispered.

Ferrand smiled. 'Yes. This is the key to their power and I want it.'

'Did you not find the crystal with it?' Mark asked; his interest was stirred.

Ferrand laughed and threw the silk cover back over it. 'I didn't do the dig. A rather wealthy Englishman did.'

'I'm surprised he parted with it,' Mark retorted.

'Let's say I had to encourage him to give it to me.'

'Like you're encouraging me?' Mark glanced over to Jane.

Ferrand laughed harder and walked back to the table. 'He had a son he was very fond of, but he didn't believe my threat to kill his son, so I sent him a message.'

Jane shivered just thinking about what Ferrand may have sent the poor father.

Ferrand smiled. 'His son lives. Fortunately for the boy, his father acted swiftly.'

'You didn't kill him?' Jane said aloud what she was thinking without realising it.

'No point. Complete waste of money. I got what I wanted.'

Jane stared at him and the look he returned gave her no satisfaction the same would apply to them. Instinctively, she knew that Ferrand would never allow Mark to live once he got the crystal working. It would be too much of a risk to him. As for her and the children, their fate would be down to Ferrand's whim and that gave her no comfort at all.

Ferrand turned to Mark and said, 'It's time you got started.'

Mark got up and helped Jane to her feet. They followed Mac out into the hall and to the children's room.

At the door, Mark looked in at the sleeping children before turning away and taking Jane into his arms. 'It'll be okay,' he said softly.

Jane saw the sadness on his face and knew that he knew; these would most probably be the last few days of his life. She hugged him tightly, hanging on to his warmth and love, trying to focus on the present moment and forcing her mind to block out any thoughts about the future.

Mac eased her and Mark apart and firmly moved her into the room. As he closed the door, he said, 'I'll bring you some food soon.'

The door lock clicked and Jane sank to the floor, her tears overwhelming her. She sobbed quietly, her thoughts searching for and not finding any speck of hope in the whirlpool of her despair.

Later that evening Mac returned with food and water. He also brought some antiseptic cream, which he applied to Jane's hand before bandaging it. He worked silently and methodically.

Jane studied him while he worked. He was very much like Stan: a hard man who had seen hard times. She also remembered the way he looked at the children and knew there was some softness in him.

He tied a perfect knot on the bandage and looked up.

She smiled at him. 'You've done this before.'

Mac nodded.

'Military?'

Mac nodded again.

'So how did you get caught up with a man like Ferrand?'

Mac got up and began to move to the door.

'You know what's happening is wrong, don't you? Please help us.'

Mac left the room, locking the door behind him.

Jane slumped against the wall. It had been worth a try. But what could she do now?

Her gaze drifted to the boarded-up window. She had already looked it over and knew she couldn't prise the wood away, and even if she could, the window had thick bars on the outside. Thicker than the ones covering the adjoining bathroom window.

She yawned and looked at the camp bed Mac had put up for her. It was so inviting that she moved over to it and slipped fully dressed under the quilt. Tomorrow she'd have to relook at what, if anything, she could do to escape this place.

CHAPTER THIRTEEN

The next day Jane busied herself playing with the children. They had been curious about her bandaged hand, but had been persuaded it was the result of another accident.

She was sitting amongst the toys watching Jamie speed a car around a road system printed on a mat. He made screeching noises as the car he was holding in one hand narrowly missed colliding with another he held in his other hand. He seemed completely immersed in his imaginary game.

Sophie was sitting between Jane's legs, surrounded by soft, cuddly toys. She was picking each one up, kissing them on their noses, then offering them to Jane to kiss too. Jane bent forward and kissed the loopy-eared teddy for the fifth time.

The lock clicked and the door opened. Mac came in with a tray full of snacks and drinks.

Sophie immediately snuggled into Jane's chest, hiding her face from him.

Jamie sat up straight and looked at what was on the tray.

Mac put the tray on the floor by Jane and took a small biscuit off the plate. He offered it to Sophie, but she refused to take it. Jane took it from him and gave it to her. Sophie immediately lost her shyness and began to munch away on it.

Jane noticed Mac was again watching the children with a gentle expression. He offered Jamie the plate and the boy took a chocolate bar.

Jane touched Mac's arm as he put the plate down. 'How's Mark?' she asked softly. 'I mean Adrian.'

Mac paused for a moment then said, 'He's working on the crystal.'

'Can I see him sometime today?'

He hesitated as if unsure what to say.

'It would be good for the children and for him,' Jane added quickly.

'I'll see what I can do.' He stood swiftly.

'Thank you,' Jane said to his back as he left.

Once the door was closed, Jamie paused eating his chocolate bar and said, 'Will we be going home soon?'

Jane didn't know how to answer him, so she said, 'Soon; it will be soon. Now who's for a drink?'

★ ★ ★

The afternoon came and went. They were served dinner by another man, who just pushed the tray through the open door onto the floor. Jane didn't get to see his face.

Sophie ate very little and refused to get off Jane's lap. Little whimpers kept coming from her.

Jane was concerned. 'What's up, little one?'

Sophie didn't answer her; instead, Jamie said, 'She's missing Mummy.'

Jane drew Sophie into her and gave her a cuddle.

'Mummy's not coming back, is she?'

Jamie's question took Jane by surprise. What could she say? Did she have any right to tell them what had happened to their mother? She took a deep breath and closed her eyes for a moment. She didn't want to lie to them, but what should she say? No, she couldn't tell them. Not here and not now. A little white lie wouldn't hurt, would it, not in situations like this? She opened her eyes and saw that Jamie and Sophie were watching her. 'I don't know wha…'

Jamie touched her face, breaking into her words and making her stop. 'It's okay,' he said softly. 'You can be our mummy until she comes back.'

Jane forced back the tears that wanted to explode into her eyes. These children seemed to have a sense about things. They seemed to know. 'O… kay,' Jane croaked and cleared it with a cough. 'What shall we play now?'

* * *

At 8pm, Sophie was sucking her thumb and searching for her toy rabbit. Jamie was helping Jane to pack away the toys. The door opened and Mac entered with Mark.

Jane's heart swelled in her chest and she so wanted to jump up and go to him, but she held back.

Jamie bounced to his feet and rushed over. 'Daddy, Daddy.'

Mark scooped him up and spun him around. His giggles were infectious and made Jane smile.

Sophie momentarily stopped her search for her rabbit and without thinking, rushed over to join in. Mark lifted her up with one arm and spun her around with Jamie. She threw her head back and screeched with delight.

Mark stopped turning and gently lowered himself to the floor, letting the children nestle into him. He was filled with so much happiness he kept kissing their heads every opportunity he could. 'Have you been having fun?' he asked softly.

The children nodded.

'Have you been good for Jane?'

Again they nodded.

'But we miss you,' Jamie said reproachfully. 'Where have you been?'

'Daddy has to do some work, but it will be done soon.' Mark looked over to Jane and nodded his appreciation to her.

'Read us a story,' Jamie demanded.

Mark quickly looked back to Mac who was standing in the doorway. He nodded and said, 'You have half an hour.' Then left.

'Okay, which one?'

Jamie chose a book and gave it to him before settling down on his father's lap with Sophie. Mark looked at the title on the front. 'The Brave Little Mouse,' he said and opened the book. Before he could continue, Jamie jumped up and ran over to Jane. He offered her his hand.

Jane didn't want to interrupt the precious moments Mark was having with his children, so she hesitated.

'Yes, Jane, come and join us,' Mark said quickly.

Jamie smiled, grabbed her hand and pulled her over to where Mark and Sophie were sitting. She settled down next to him, allowing room for Jamie to sit between them.

'Right, let's begin.'

★ ★ ★

All too soon, Mac was back and signalling for Mark to leave. Sophie had fallen asleep in Mark's arms and he gently put her into her bed, kissing her gently on the forehead. He took Jamie's hand and led him to the other bed, tucking him in and kissing him goodnight too. As he went to leave, Jamie said, 'I love you, Daddy.'

Mark touched Jamie's head and said, 'And I love you too, so very much. Sleep now.'

Jane was standing by the door and as he reached her, she saw him look back at the children and wipe his fingers across his eyes. He turned to her and she took him into her arms. There was nothing to say.

Mac coughed, then said, 'Let's go.'

Mark eased her body away, cupped her face in his hands and kissed her tenderly. When he pulled back he said, 'I love you.'

Mac took his arm and they left.

Jane held her hands to her stomach. The emptiness had returned and the fear she would never see him again festered in her mind. She desperately wanted them all to leave this place, but there was no way of escaping.

CHAPTER FOURTEEN

That night Jane tossed and turned. Every time she closed her eyes, her mind would replay Solita's killing, the burning of her hand, and then her imagination would play out numerous possible ways Ferrand would kill them. She snapped open her eyes at the point of her fifth death and took a deep breath.

This was madness. She needed to sleep to be there for the children in the morning, but she couldn't bear to close her eyes and experience her mind's brutality any longer. She finally decided to meditate and call in her guides, Spirit Wind and Swaying Tree, to help her.

Jane tentatively closed her eyes, focusing on her breath and imagining she was at the edge of the forest. In an instant she was there and both her guides were waiting for her.

Spirit Wind smiled as she approached and she noticed that in the smile there was warmth and compassion. His weathered, tanned face hadn't changed and his Native American attire, including the feathered headdress, was the same, but something about him was different. She put it down to his demeanour, which seemed more caring and outward than in her previous encounters with him.

He moved towards her and took hold of her hand.

Surprised, she looked into his brown eyes and found a well of love. It was quite overpowering and she took a deep breath.

Spirit Wind said, 'You are close to the end now, Jane.'

His words shook her and she swallowed hard. 'We are going to die!'

Once she had stated it, all fear seemed to disperse as if at last she was resigning herself to it.

Spirit Wind laughed. 'Not just yet.'

She looked at him, confused. 'Then what end are you referring to?'

He patted her hand. 'The end to an action that created this world...' He fell quiet before adding, '...From what it should have been. Do you have the courage and strength to finish this?'

Jane didn't hesitate. 'Yes.'

Spirit Wind let go of her hand and turned away. 'Then it is time to show you the past event that needs to be resolved.'

Jane looked to Swaying Tree and saw him nod and beckon her to join them. She moved over to him.

He waited until they were walking side by side before speaking. 'Spirit Wind will take you to an event in your past and you will see what has happened, which continues to affect your life and the lives of others in this lifetime.'

She saw his young face become serious. 'What is it? What's wrong?'

'You will see and experience the events through your own eyes and you may not like what you see.'

'So what do I have to do?'

Swaying Tree pondered for a moment. 'I do not know. It is for you to see what action has been taken and consider how to change it.'

Spirit Wind stopped by a clearing where a campfire was already lit within a circle of stones. He turned to her. 'These events are currently unfolding in this lifetime and once you know what happened in the past, you will be able to change the way the action is taken now.'

'So I can change what happened in the past in this lifetime?'

Spirit Wind nodded. 'This is your chance, but it may be difficult for you to see what you have to do. Be alert, trust your instincts and you will succeed.'

'And if I don't succeed?' Jane sensed the uneasiness in him and felt the weight of impending doom fill the silence around them. She didn't wait for his answer. 'Okay, but will I get a second chance?'

Both guides slowly shook their heads.

'No! So if I fail, things will end in the same way?' She didn't need to see their head nods to know she was right. She took a big breath. Could she really do this?

Spirit Wind and Swaying Tree moved into the circle and she sat between them. They offered her their hands and she felt a warm tingle flow into her as she connected with them. It took several deep breaths to clear her mind of her doubts and fear that seemed ready to overwhelm her. Finally, she relaxed, and a moment later she was in a beautiful city of low white marble buildings…

★ ★ ★

It was pleasantly warm and the sun was shining in a clear blue sky. Areas of lush green grass surrounded each building and were filled with colourful flowers and shaded by green-leaved trees. In the centre of the city was a pyramid.

At first, Jane thought she was in Egypt, but then she noticed the people. There were white and dark-skinned humans, wandering around the streets, dressed in bright clothes that looked like silk. Some of the white people had long, dark hair and wore robes that hung from their shoulders, tied at the waist with a golden cord. Just like the dress she saw herself wearing in her vision at the temple of Apollo in Greece. Others, including those that were dark-skinned, wore cloaks over a tunic and trousers and carried staffs that were topped with crystal points. Everyone looked happy and peaceful.

She was dressed in a white and gold robe that fastened at each shoulder and was pulled in at the waist with a golden clasp in the shape of the sun. On her feet she wore brown sandals and in her hair she had golden clips. She somehow knew she was a person of high regard and respect, maybe a priestess.

She moved through the cobbled streets, acknowledging the greetings others gave her, until she came to a marbled building slightly bigger than the rest. It had an archway opening to the inside where a white man with blond hair was standing. He was dressed in the same way as her. Jane sensed he was a priest too and that this building was like a temple.

She removed her shoes and he offered her his hand to guide her inside. The floor was made of white and dark marble slabs and cool on her bare feet. The walls were of white stone with flecks of gold embedded in it, which glinted in the sunlight that was coming from the open space where the roof should have been. The inner part of the temple was completely open to the elements and in the centre was an altar. A ten-foot quartz crystal point was suspended in mid-air above it and she could see no hanging attachments or poles to secure it.

When she reached the altar, there was a golden amulet in its centre in the shape of an elongated circle. The carvings on the amulet looked like a basic butterfly shape. It had four discs encased in a circle for its head, with two antennae projecting from the top. Attached to the side of the head was a wing shape which was split into four. Two curvy lines ran down behind the butterfly at the narrowest end of the whole amulet.

Jane recognised it and a memory that had been buried surfaced. The symbol on the amulet represented the creator and the sacred four. Its meaning was: *By command of the Creator, the Sacred Four will establish Law and Order throughout the universe.* She instinctively knew she was a teacher of the sacred words of their motherland, but had no memory of what they were.

Two white men hurriedly approached. One had shoulder-length grey hair and was dressed the same way as the priest except that his robe was a creamy grey colour. The other man was much younger, his blond hair shorter and he wore a pale cream tunic over trousers.

The older man spoke first. 'Something must be done; he is meddling in things that should be left alone.' He stroked his clean-shaven chin and his deep blue eyes looked at her pleadingly.

The younger man responded before Jane could say anything. 'But Seer Lamar, we advance ourselves by trying out new things.'

The old man turned on him. 'That may be so, Thorus; but what he is doing is cruel and it won't keep him from utilising others as he sees fit.'

Jane could see the wisdom and youth combination in them: the master and the apprentice, but she wished she knew what they were talking about.

The old man spoke directly to her. 'It must stop. You are aware Marcus has been spending time with him.'

The priest, who had brought her into the temple,

interrupted. 'Seer Lamar, you must not worry so. Soljana has taught Marcus well. She will advise him of the influence Ferrus is having on him.'

Jane now knew her name was Soljana.

Lamar moved round the altar to stand beside her. 'Please, Priestess of Ra, just look into it for us. Guide Marcus away from Ferrus, for I fear bad things will come about.'

Jane took his hands in hers and when she spoke her voice was sweet and angelic. 'Lamar, do not let your thoughts dwell on such worry. It will create what you fear.'

Lamar nodded. 'As you wish, my Priestess.'

She turned to the priest and said, 'I want to see Marcus. Where is he?'

He nodded towards the pyramid, which stood behind the temple.

Jane followed him to the back archway and down some steps to the street behind the temple. Several people smiled at her as she passed by and it wasn't long before they reached the pyramid. It was gleaming in the sunlight for its silver-coloured walls had a striking mosaic pattern made from coloured gemstones. The priest stopped at the archway entrance and allowed her to go in alone.

It was bright inside the pyramid and Jane noticed that its pointed top was not connected, leaving an opening to the sky where the sun's rays could stream down in shafts of light. In the centre directly under the open top was a tripod, holding a large double-pointed quartz crystal.

This one was different to the crystal Mark used in Africa. Two of its sides were narrow and slightly obscure while the other four sides were perfectly clear. Somehow, Jane knew it was a Lemurian crystal from their motherland. When Jane got closer she saw that the tripod was the same style as the one Ferrand had, but it was much bigger and there was no Vesica Piscis in the centre.

Standing behind the crystal was a young man and when he turned to her she recognised him; it was Mark. A well of love filled her heart and she had to stop herself from running to him.

'Mark,' Jane called without thinking and when he frowned, she quickly corrected herself: 'Marcus.'

He smiled and moved to greet her, kissing her gently on the cheek. 'Soljana, it's always lovely to have you visit.'

His manner was polite, but the twinkle in his eyes reflected his excitement at seeing her. She sensed that the love between them was so sacred that it had to remain hidden and she wondered if it had anything to do with her position in the temple.

'What are you doing today?' she asked as casually as she could.

'Come, come. I have made progress.' He took her to an area set back from the main room at the far end of the pyramid and pulled out another tripod.

This one was exactly the same as the one Ferrand had.

'I've made some adjustments and here I've made the connection between Spirit and Matter.' He pointed to the Vesica Piscis in the centre, the oval shape made by two overlapping circles. He quickly pulled out a silk bag from a basket nearby. 'And, I've made this.'

From the bag he took out a clear crystal point. It had twelve perfectly angled sides. One end of the crystal was wide and tapered to a point while the other end came to a narrow, very precise point. The sunlight caught it, making it shine so brightly that Jane had to look away.

'What does it do?' she asked.

Marcus couldn't contain his excitement. 'When I place the large end in the sacred oval, it is programmed to send earth energy to the source of all that is – our home; and when I reverse it, it brings our home energy to earth.'

'But our current one does this already in a balanced way.'

'Yes, yes, but this crystal will amplify the energy. Its shape allows the energy to magnify itself as it goes through the crystal and come out in a more powerful, focused beam.'

'Why would we need it?' Jane asked, her concern growing.

Marcus shrugged his shoulders and a voice behind her said, 'It will also allow us to control the "Things" by disrupting their energy field.'

The hairs on Jane's neck and skin prickled. She knew the voice and turned to find Ferrand standing behind her.

'Ferrus,' Marcus said urgently, 'it hasn't been tested for that.'

'No, not yet.'

'We would not need anything to control the "Things" if you hadn't created them in the first place,' Jane said coldly.

Ferrus moved closer and Jane stepped back. 'I was only helping our citizens to experience their animalistic side.'

'But it has gone too far,' Jane scolded.

Ferrus walked around her, smiling. 'You have nothing to worry about, my priestess; I'll protect you.' He touched her hair and Jane moved away.

He laughed and slapped Marcus on the back. 'Your apprentice is doing well, Soljana.' He looked at the crystal. 'But Marcus, I think you need to make a better one than this, a more powerful one.'

'NO!' Jane shouted. 'The crystals are healing tools and they help us bring balance to the world. Marcus, you must remember this.'

Marcus looked at her and then Ferrus. He looked disappointed as he nodded in reply to her instruction.

Ferrus whispered something to him. Jane didn't hear and his face lightened a moment.

'As you wish,' Ferrus said, a hint of sarcasm in his voice. He turned away, muttering something else to Marcus.

'Ferrus,' Jane called to him. He turned his head to look at her. 'No more experiments with the "Things".'

He laughed. 'You have no power to control me. Our leader, Prime Sun Ra, has said we must do what we have to do to help please the citizens and that is exactly what I'm doing.' He walked out of the pyramid before she could say anything else.

★ ★ ★

In the next moment, Jane found herself in another beautiful building made of marble. Again, there was no roof and the position of the sun overhead bathed the room with light. In the centre was another altar and this time the golden amulet upon it was in the shape of a square. Carved into the amulet was a different symbol. An almost closed square was in the centre of a circle and around the circle were four blades, one in each of the directions, north, east, south and west. The points of the blades were curved to the right and attached to the right side of each of them was an arrowhead. Inscribed on each of the blades was a symbol that looked like the side view of two deep steps.

Standing a few feet away from the altar a tall, incredibly handsome man in a golden gown tied at the waist with a golden band. His slightly elongated head was covered in blond hair and his tanned face was wrinkle-free. Somehow, she knew he was quite old, maybe even older than human years allowed, but his appearance was of a man only thirty. As she approached him, he smiled.

'Soljana,' he said softly and with fondness, his voice sweet like a bird's song. He kissed her cheek. 'You have brightened my day.'

His words were nectar to her ears, soothing her emotions and bringing a warm glow to her whole body. He took her hand and they walked back to the altar.

Everything felt good and blissful in his presence and Jane was so content she forgot where she was and why she had come. He let go of her hand and her dreamy state vanished.

'How can I help you?' he asked.

Jane had to really think hard about why she was there and when the memory came, it brought worry and fear with it. She reluctantly let it intrude on the wonderful way she was feeling.

'Prime Sun Ra, Seer Lamar is deeply worried about what Ferrus is doing with the citizens. His experiments are not good.'

Sun Ra stood for a moment in thought before replying. 'Ferrus is only doing what the citizens have requested.'

'But is it right?' Jane pushed.

Sun Ra touched the amulet. 'The creator with his four primary forces made this world. He created us as part of himself so that we may experience this world as we see fit.'

'But what Ferrus is doing is beyond this.' Jane could feel her tension rising.

Sun Ra smiled. 'I think as part of the creator we must try out different things, so we can relay the experiences back.'

'But it's so cruel.'

'The citizens who volunteer want to experience their

animal instincts; he has to make changes so they can do this.'

'Yes, but once he has finished with them, they become aggressive. They snarl and bite. They are not happy and he cannot undo what he has done, so they become a problem.'

'I think you have taken on Seer Lamar's worry, Soljana.'

Jane shook her head. 'The experiments are changing the creator's original design; is that right?'

Sun Ra came over to her and touched her lightly on the shoulder.

Immediately, her frustration and tension disappeared and were replaced by contentment and peace.

He smiled again. 'I will take this back to the creator. Our purpose is to live with love and happiness. Don't let fear and worry come into your life.'

She smiled at him. 'Thank you.'

Sun Ra's ability to connect to their home – the source of all that is – filled him with the goodness that came directly from the creator. Jane knew all would be well and she left him feeling wonderful and at peace with herself and everyone else.

★ ★ ★

Jane's vision seemed to refocus for a moment and when it returned there was chaos happening around her. People were running around frantically, screaming in terror, fear etched on their faces. Cloaked guardians were fighting in the street with half-animal, half-human beings.

Jane found herself close to the temple and rushed up the steps out of the way. The air was filled with panic and terror and it seeped into her skin, making her shiver. She moved inside, but the screams and snarls followed her, echoing loudly through the open archways. With her heart beating wildly, Jane ran to the altar to find some comfort.

Lamar rushed in, followed by Thorus.

'The "Things" are out of control. The guardians are having trouble pushing them out of the city,' Lamar yelled above the noise.

Jane nodded.

'But there is a bigger problem.'

The floor shook beneath their feet and Jane clung to the altar for support, quickly glancing at the crystal above it, which hadn't moved.

'Ferrus is with Marcus in the pyramid. He plans to use the new crystal Marcus has created to destroy the "Things", but it will do worse than that.'

'What will it do?' Jane yelled as the floor shook again.

Lamar came closer and grasped her arm. 'Marcus has special skills he is only just aware of. He can directly connect with the energy of the universe, and his new crystal is capable of amplifying that energy and transmitting it into anything he programs it to.' The old man took a breath and continued, 'There is a cosmic star approaching. It will come near our world. If he brings down the energy in conjunction with the cosmic star's energy, it will magnify everything. It will kill him and overbear the earth herself, creating a catastrophe.'

'What can we do?' Jane gripped the altar more tightly as the earth shook again.

'You must stop him. He will listen to you.'

Jane looked at each of the men in turn. 'I will do my best.'

She left the temple by the back archway and went out into the street. At the bottom of the steps she abruptly stopped. People were lying on the cobbles, some dead, others dying. Their blood seeping along the mortar channels like tiny rivers.

Several guardians were helping others limp their way to the steps of the temple, their arms and legs scared with deep claw marks.

She felt a huge heaviness in her heart and a twisting in her stomach. The memory of Sun Ra's touch unable to shift the fear and anguish her body was holding.

She moved away from the steps, swiftly past the guardians, only barely noticing that one had stopped to watch her. She raised her robe above her ankles as she skipped from dry cobble to dry cobble to avoid the blood.

Just as she reached the steps of the pyramid, something large and hairy lunged at her from the right. She screamed, twisting away to her left.

Claws with razor sharp edges slashed into her right arm and she slipped on the blood-coated cobbles, falling heavily.

The beast was upon her. Its thick, padded front feet thumping hard onto her shoulders, forcing her down onto the ground.

Jane stared with horror into the snarling bear-snouted face of the Thing.

'NO… OOO…' Jane screamed as it bent down to rip at her face.

It faltered for a moment.

Jane could see puzzlement in its human's eyes; maybe some recognition of what it was doing had registered in the human part of its brain.

The next moment it drew back its lips in a snarl, exposing long, sharp teeth and lunged at her throat.

At that moment a crystal-tipped staff swung down onto the Thing's head and smashed its skull into two. It died instantly, its body collapsing onto her.

Jane gasped in shock as its weight landed on her body and

her stomach heaved at the strong smell of blood coming from the Thing's mouth, now resting on her neck. She frantically squirmed and twisted her body, pushing with her hands and kicking with her legs in a bid to get it off her.

A pair of leather-gloved hands gripped the Thing's black, furry back and pushed its body to one side.

Jane looked up at the guardian who had saved her, but he turned his attention away, alert to anything else that may come from the side street by the pyramid.

She got up quickly, wiping the beast's blood from her hands onto her blood-soaked robe. 'Thank you,' she mumbled and rushed up the steps to the pyramid.

Inside, she paused for a moment to compose herself. Her right arm hurt like mad and the stench of blood was heavy in her nose. She took a few breaths to settle her stomach before making her way to the centre.

In the place where the original crystal had stood was Marcus' new tripod and a new, bright, two-foot-high pulsing crystal was nestled inside. Jane could tell by the way it felt that this was more powerful than the other had been. It was also not the shaped crystal Marcus had shown her, but a crystal with an even point at each end, clearer and more precise than any crystal she had seen.

Marcus was finely adjusting its position so its top point was under the opening of the pyramid top and its bottom directly over a hole in the ground where the original shaped crystal Marcus had made was positioned. Its wide end facing upwards and its narrow end pointing into the earth.

Jane rushed over to him. 'Stop, stop, you'll destroy us all.'

Marcus looked up, surprised. 'No, it will help...' He stopped, registering the state she was in. 'What happened to you?'

'Never mind about that. You have to stop.'

'But I made it so it will help.'

Jane grabbed his arm. 'No, it won't. Lamar says there is a star approaching. It will cause destruction if you activate it now.'

'Don't listen to her, boy.' Ferrus stepped in between them, pushing Jane away. 'Remember the tests.'

Marcus nodded. 'Yes, Soljana, the tests were great. We managed to disrupt the Things' energy patterns and it made them remember who they were. It gave them some of their humanness back.'

Jane showed him her arm. 'I've just been attacked by one and seen it remember, but it only lasts a few moments. It would have killed me if a guardian hadn't saved me.'

'But I can enhance it. I have a gift that Ferrus helped me find. I can control the universal power and enhance the effects of the crystal.'

'No, Marcus. The energy will be too strong; trust me.'

Marcus hesitated.

'Trust me,' Jane said again.

Marcus nodded. 'Maybe she's right, Ferrus.'

Jane was suddenly grabbed from behind. The grip was firm and strong. It was a guardian and Jane just caught a glimpse of the lower part of his face. She seemed to recognise it.

'She's in danger,' Ferrus said quickly. 'Take her to the temple.'

Jane struggled against the grip forcing her away. 'No, Marcus, please.'

Ferrus turned to Marcus. 'You can save her, but we need to do it now.'

As Jane was dragged to the archway, she saw Marcus turn back to the crystal and knew she had lost.

Back at the temple, Lamar stared at her in fear as she stumbled in. 'What are you doing back here?' he yelled.

'Marcus won't stop and one of the guardians brought me here for safety.'

Lamar grabbed her forearm. 'You shouldn't be here. You need to go back.' He began rushing her back to the archway.

At that moment there was a massive flash of light.

Jane shielded her face to protect her eyes from its effect.

The air around them sizzled as if an electric current had energised the air and she fell to the floor, feeling sick and weak.

A deep rumble rippled through the floor and Jane dropped her hands to see. Her vision was obscured as if she was looking through a steamed-up window.

The floor heaved upwards, cracking the marble and raising it three feet. The altar toppled over and the suspended crystal above it crashed to the floor, splitting into thousands of fragments that flew all around her. None touched her.

Her vision cleared and she saw Lamar laying close by. He had taken a crystal shaft to his chest. Thorus was lying alongside him with a pale face and blank expression. He was staring at a pool of blood seeping from Lamar towards him.

Jane crawled over the shuddering floor until she reached them; only then did she see that Thorus had been cut in two and his life had gone. She took Lamar's hand. He was coughing blood as he tried to say something to her.

'I can't hear you,' she said, raising her voice as more thunderous noises came from outside.

She looked through the archway and saw houses crumbling into cavernous holes appearing in the earth. She moved her head closer to his face.

'You could have saved us,' he gurgled.

'How?' Jane yelled, 'what could I have done? Tell me.'

But it was too late. Lamar had died.

The floor undulated again, sending her scrambling for a flatter, more stable piece of marble. Lamar and Thorus' bodies were swallowed by the earth.

Outside, the land was shaking and cracking open violently; pockets of fire and hot rock were flying into the air. She saw the Things running frantically in all directions, some even into the fiery pits they were trying to avoid.

She saw an opportunity to reach the pyramid and ran as fast and as carefully as she could. Stepping over hot boulders and leaping over holes that suddenly spilt open in front of her. She flung herself into the pyramid as the front archway collapsed.

Inside, the destruction was the same as that of the temple. The floor was broken apart and the interior walls were crumbling down around her.

She saw Marcus lying close to the centre where the tripod and crystal had been. The crystal had shattered and the tripod had disappeared, but the crystal in the earth was still pulsating and glowing. She could feel its vibration hitting her body, throwing her off balance, draining her energy. Her body's energy centres were twisting and turning in different directions, making her feel ill. She dropped to the floor and crawled to where Marcus was lying.

He was shallow breathing and unaware that most of his torso and lower body had disintegrated. Jane turned his face to her and the flesh of his cheek melted on her fingers.

'I'm so sorry,' he mouthed to her, as he couldn't speak.

Jane shook her head as tears rushed down her cheeks.

'I only wanted to help,' he mouthed again.

'I know…' Jane whispered. 'I love you so much.'

He smiled a content smile and died.

'No. No…' Jane cried, not wanting to let him go. Their love had been so special she could not bear to think she was never going to see him again.

The earth rumbled around her again and she grabbed a piece of raised marble to stop from falling into a crack that opened up beneath her, swallowing the remains of Marcus' body.

A movement from across the way caught her eye. It was the hooded guardian that had taken her to the temple earlier. He was heading for the only archway exit that was still unblocked. In his arms he was carrying the tripod Marcus had created.

At the exit she spotted Ferrus on the floor. He was covered in blood from several wounds made by crystal shards, especially a large one that had penetrated his chest, but he was still alive. He got to his hands and knees and crawled out of the pyramid.

She turned her attention back to the guardian. 'Wait!' she yelled.

He stopped at the archway and looked back at her. There was hesitation, as if he was considering returning for her, but he continued on and disappeared.

Jane scrambled up the upheaved mound of floor until she was clear of the hole and rested against a large upright piece. A new noise was approaching. It had a soft kind of rumble and a swishing, hissing sound. The ground again shuddered and as the earth began to sink beneath her, she saw the approaching wave of water. In that moment, before she died, she suddenly knew the face of the guardian; it was Stan.

CHAPTER FIFTEEN

Jane felt her hand being squeezed and her consciousness return to the circle and her guides. She sat silently for a while, her mind trying to process all she had seen. It had been terrible. She could still feel the effects of the crystal's vibrations on her body and smell the fire and dust that had surrounded her. Tears she hadn't known she had been holding began to flow down her face as she remembered Marcus' death. And on top of it all, she felt burdened with guilt because she could have saved them. It weighed heavily on her for she still didn't know what she should have done or what she needed to do now in this timeline to change it. She sighed deeply.

Spirit Wind handed her a cup of fluid. 'This will help,' he said.

She drank the sweet liquid and after a moment her body felt better and the sickness subsided. 'Was I in Atlantis?' she finally asked.

'Yes,' Spirit Wind said, 'and you've had many lives before and after that one.'

'But I couldn't stop it. I didn't find out what I needed to do.'

Spirit Wind gently looked at her. 'It will become clearer in time.'

'Why now? Why this lifetime? Didn't this opportunity happen before now?'

Spirit Wind pondered for a moment. 'All things must be connected,' he said to himself. He turned to her as realisation came to him. 'The main elements did not come together until this lifetime.'

'Elements, what elements?'

Swaying Tree spoke softly. 'The elements that caused the destruction of the mighty city.'

'Do you mean me, Mark, Ferrand and Stan?'

Spirit Wind shook his head. 'You, Mark, Ferrand, Stan and the star.'

'There's a star approaching?'

Both her guides nodded.

Jane sighed again. The weight on her shoulders settling even more heavily.

Spirit Wind stood up and Jane got up too. His eyes were softly focusing on her. 'We have trust in you, Jane.' Then he turned and walked away.

She watched him go and wished she had that same faith in herself.

Swaying Tree touched her arm and they walked together to the edge of the forest.

When she got there, she looked at the beautiful meadow before her, feeling the warm sunshine on her face. How she wished she could just stay here and forget about what was happening in the real world. It was so frightening not knowing what Ferrand was going to do to them. Now, on top of it all, she had this past-life event occurring too.

Her mind wanted to dismiss it, make her believe that it was just a load of made-up nonsense, but another part of her knew this was as real as what she was going back to.

She was here, at this moment in time, because of what had happened in the past; and somehow she needed to resolve both the past and her current situation without herself and everyone else being killed.

She gave another big sigh. This burden she was carrying seemed just too much. She didn't know what to do, yet so much was relying on her doing it right this time.

Swaying Tree said softly, 'Trust yourself and Spirit will guide you.' He smiled and walked away.

Jane came back from her meditation. The room was dark and she could hear the soft breathing of the children as they slept.

The past-life events were still vivid in her mind and she fast forwarded them to the end.

As she crunched the pillow into shape and nestled her head into it she thought, *But what part does Stan play in all of this?*

★ ★ ★

Jane woke with a head that felt like it was filled with bricks. The images of Atlantis had replayed in her dreams and she hadn't slept well. Jamie and Sophie were playing quietly, but when they noticed she was awake they came over to her.

Sophie touched Jane's puffy eyes with her tiny fingers.

'We heard you moaning and crying in your sleep,' Jamie said, 'was it a bad dream?'

Jane smiled. 'Yes, it was a bad dream. Have you washed?'

Jamie nodded.

Sophie took hold of her hand. 'You want to come with me?' Sophie nodded and Jane whisked her up into her arms before walking into the adjourning bathroom. The bars on the only window still caught her eye every time she entered the room, reminding her of her captivity.

Jane rinsed her face with water and took the towel from Sophie who was patiently waiting by the sink. The towel was soft and fresh and she buried her face into it, rubbing the tiredness from her eyes. Her mind kept thinking about the events of the night. She needed to speak to Mark about it. Perhaps she could get him to stop making the crystal. She lifted her head from the towel and looked at Sophie. *But at what cost?*

She put the towel on the rail and they both returned to the mat where Jamie was playing.

The door opened and Mac came in with their breakfasts. He placed the tray by the children and was walking away when Jane intercepted him. 'I need to see Mark, urgently.'

Mac stopped and looked back at the children.

'It's not the children.'

He shook his head.

'Please, I just need a few moments alone with him.'

Mac seemed to hesitate, then said, 'Lunchtime. I'll come for you.'

Jane smiled. 'Thank you.'

He just turned away and left.

★ ★ ★

Just before noon, Mac returned and took Jane down the corridor to a room at the end of the house. There was a guard on the door who opened it as they got to him. Inside was a small laboratory with a central working area running the whole length of the room.

Mark was working at the far end when she and Mac entered. He looked up, surprised to see her, then rushed over. 'What's happened?'

'Nothing, the children are fine.'

The relief on his face was instant.

'I just needed to see you.'

He smiled and took her in his arms.

They held each other, seemingly oblivious to all around them, but Jane heard Mac step out of the room and close the door. When she heard the click of the door-lock, she pulled away from Mark. 'I've had a vision of Atlantis. My guides have shown me what will happen if you continue to make the crystal.'

She took hold of his hand and walked him to the window in the wall furthest away from the door. In a whispered voice, she relayed as quickly as she could the events in Atlantis.

Mark listened intently until she finished. He moved over to the bench and pulled out a stool to sit on. For a minute he just stared at the floor, then he said, 'You are telling me that I created the crystal that caused the destruction of Atlantis.' His voice was soft but shaky. 'And you're now asking me to believe that what I am doing here could result in destruction too?'

Jane took hold of his hands. 'Yes.'

'Why should it?'

'Because of the approaching star.'

He shook his head. 'I know the crystal is powerful, but I brought the universal energy down into it before and it worked all right in Africa. Why not here?'

Jane gripped his hands tighter. 'I think if you do this with the closeness of the star, it will destroy you, and maybe all of us.'

Mark pulled one of his hands away and took something from his pocket. It was the crystal pyramid. He showed it to her. 'This kept me safe; it stopped the energy from absorbing me. It should work again.'

Jane could feel panic in her body. Mark seemed determined

to carry on making the crystal. She needed him to believe her. 'But what if it doesn't? What if the star's energy is too powerful?'

Mark stood up and began to pace the room.

Jane watched him.

Finally, he stopped and looked at her. 'I can't see my children or you hurt. I have no choice but to continue, even if I didn't want to.'

Jane rushed over to him. 'But we could all die if you do. You can't trust Ferrand to let us go when it has been done. Please, Mark.' She could see she was losing him, so she said, 'You promised me you wouldn't give Ferrand the crystal. Mark, please, I'm so scared.'

He pulled her into him and hugged her tightly.

The door opened and Mac beckoned her back to him.

She kissed Mark long and hard on the lips for she feared this may be her only opportunity to be this close to him again and as she gently eased back, she cupped his face in her hands. 'I love you.'

Mark put his hands over hers and gently brought them down to his chest. He squeezed them and whispered, 'I'll think of something. Go now… Don't worry.'

Jane left with Mac and returned to the children. She watched them playing with the cars, laughing and giggling.

Her spirit was low with what she had asked Mark to do. There was a big risk that Ferrand would seriously hurt them if Mark stopped working, but there was also a big risk to all of them if Mark continued. It just seemed so hopeless.

Jamie rushed up to her and took her hand. 'Come play with us?'

Jane forced herself to smile. How she wished she could be like the children, oblivious to the danger they were in. 'Okay, what do you want to play?'

***

Later that afternoon there was a commotion outside their room. Jane could hear raised voices and one was Ferrand's. She quickly moved to the door, straining to hear what was being said.

Mac's deep tone came first. 'I'm not happy about this. Can't we…'

Ferrand cut him off. 'I don't care if you're happy or not. Just do it.'

'Can't you do this another way?'

'No, just bring them, NOW,' Ferrand snapped back.

The door-lock clicked and Jane swiftly moved away to stand by the children.

Mac and another man entered. 'You need to come with us,' Mac said.

Jane moved towards him.

'And the children,' he added.

Jane suddenly became afraid. She saw the grim look on Mac's face and knew something bad was going to happen. She moved back to the children and lifted Sophie into her arms. Jamie came over to stand beside her and quietly took her hand. She hesitated. She didn't want to go.

Mac nodded towards the door where the other man was waiting.

She shook her head, forcing Mac to come to her. He caught her by the elbow and pushed her in front of him.

'What's happening?' Jane turned to him, but he just shook his head and pushed her on.

Once out of the room, they made their way towards Mark's laboratory. Jane's stomach was churning and she faltered in her step, wishing she could walk the other way,

150

but Mac's touch on her elbow ensured she and the children continued on.

They entered Mark's room.

Jane saw him stood between two other men. Ferrand was lounging on a stool next to the bench Mark had been working at.

At the sight of his father, Jamie tried to rush forward, but Jane tightened her grip on his hand. He looked at her, puzzled, then back at the scene in front of him. Instinctively, he drew closer to her.

Ferrand eased himself off the stool. 'Ah, we are all here now.' He walked up to Jane, staring into her face. She could see malaise in his eyes and her breath caught in her throat. He bent down to Jamie, and Jane could feel Jamie's hand tighten in hers.

'You see your dad there?' Ferrand said, his eyes fixed on the boy's face. 'Well he's been a naughty boy.'

Jane held her breath. She knew what was coming.

Ferrand stood up and in a flash whipped Sophie out of Jane's arms.

Jane lunged forward to grab her back, but Mac caught both her arms, pulling her into his body.

Sophie looked at her in shock, then her bottom lip began to quiver.

Jamie moved to go to her, but the other man behind him caught his shoulder hard, making him yelp.

'No, please don't hurt them,' Mark yelled, moving forward. Ferrand's men quickly restrained him.

Jane saw Ferrand grin as he turned to face Mark. 'Tell me you aren't delaying the process,' he said coldly. 'It should be done by now.'

'It's taken longer than I thought. I'll try to speed it up,' Mark said quickly.

Ferrand looked at Sophie. 'I think your daddy's lying.'

'I'm not; please, I'm not.'

Ferrand took hold of Sophie's left hand; he examined each of her fingers. 'Which of these little pinkies don't you need?'

'No. Don't hurt her. Please don't hurt her.' Mark struggled with the men holding him, but they overpowered him and pushed him to his knees. He stared up at Ferrand with wide eyes and his voice trembled. 'I… I'll do it, I'll do whatever you want, just don't hurt her.'

Ferrand took hold of her little finger.

Sophie began to whimper as if she knew what was going to happen.

'IT'S MY FAULT!' Jane shouted. 'I asked Mark to delay making the crystal. Take it out on me!'

Ferrand turned to her, gleaming with pleasure at hearing her confession. He looked at Sophie and said, 'You think she's done enough to save your finger?'

He turned his head and stared into Jane's face.

The silence was palpable.

His eyelids didn't blink and his face showed no emotion. Only the murderous blaze in his eyes betrayed his intention.

He snapped Sophie's little finger.

Her scream filled the room, followed by a bellow of screeching cries.

Jane cried with her.

Mac's grip on Jane's arms tightened to hurting point, then he released her.

Ferrand walked over and flung Sophie into Jane's arms and as she was distracted in consoling the little girl, he backhanded Jane across the face. The force of the hit sent her to her knees.

Ferrand bent over her. 'That's only the start of what I am going to do to you,' he said menacingly.

Jane ignored the stinging flesh of her cheek and concentrated on shielding Sophie from him.

'You're a horrible MAN!' Jamie yelled and instantly drew back as Ferrand faced him.

Ferrand smiled at the boy. 'I know.'

Jane watched him ponder for a second on whether he was going to do anything to the boy, but thankfully he turned away and walked over to stand in front of Mark, who was still on his knees, his head bowed down.

'Now get on with it or you'll see a lot more of this,' Ferrand said coldly.

Mark looked up.

Jane could just see him. His eyes had narrowed and his lips were pulled tightly together. The fury on his face shocked her and she quickly looked at his hands; they were pulsing red. No one else seemed to notice it.

The room was still, an eerie silence that pre-empted something coming, just like the stillness before a storm. Jane held her breath.

Ferrand moved away and Mark had direct sight of her and the children. The tension in him dissolved immediately, the fury faded to compliance and any resistance he may have had was now completely gone.

'I want it done by tomorrow noon, or for every hour after that I will hurt your kids.'

Mark just nodded.

Mac helped Jane off the floor and escorted her and the children back to their room.

Ferrand followed behind.

As the door closed behind her, she heard Mac turn on him.

'This is not what I signed up for.'

Ferrand's reply was curt. 'You don't like it? Tough. Perhaps you'd better think of your own well-being instead of theirs.'

'What does that mean?'

'No one leaves my employ unless I wish it. Understand?'

'Perfectly.' Mac's reply was firm, but not submissive.

There was a pause and Ferrand's tone softened. 'Look, Mac, soon this will be over. There are bigger things out there for us. If it really affects you to be with the children, I'll reassign you.'

'No. I'm fine.'

Ferrand laughed. 'Good, come on then, let's get a drink.'

Jane moved away from the door and sat on the bed with Sophie on her lap. The little finger was bent at a horrible angle and Sophie's crying had turned into sobs.

'We'll make it better,' Jane soothed, although she had no idea what she should do.

Jamie came and sat down beside her. His face was wet with tears.

'I… I don't like that man. He hurt Sophie.'

Jane put her arm around him and drew him in close.

★ ★ ★

Half an hour later Mac returned with a splint and a bandage. He handed Jane a cup of juice.

Sophie tried to claw her way into Jane's blouse.

'What's this?' Jane looked at the drink he had given her.

'It's a mild sedative, so she won't feel any pain when I mend the finger.'

Jane coaxed Sophie into drinking it and soon the little girl was sleeping.

Mac reset her finger as she lay on Jane's lap and bandaged it against her other fingers. Jane noticed how gentle he was and he took care in how he handled her.

Jamie was watching. He didn't speak, but Jane could see he was trying to figure out if Mac was a nice man or not.

When Mac was finished, he took a look at Jane's face. 'There's some bruising, but no other damage.'

As he withdrew his hand, she caught hold of it and whispered, 'Please help us.'

He shook his head and stood up.

Jane went to speak again but he abruptly turned and walked away.

She quickly laid Sophie on the bed and rushed after him, catching hold of his arm as he reached the door. 'Mac, please…'

Without warning, Mac turned around and pushed her hard against the wall. His face drew near hers and he said harshly, 'I can't help you.'

Jane looked into his eyes and persisted. 'Then please get a message to our friend…'

Mac closed a hand over her mouth, shutting off her words.

Jane grabbed his hand and eased it away slightly. 'His na… me is St… an,' she muffled into his hand. 'At the mo… tel.' She thought she saw him raise an eyebrow.

'I told you I can't help you. Just pray your boyfriend does his job in time.'

As he took his hand from her mouth, she thought she saw him wink, but then he was gone.

Jane returned to the bed and sat down.

Jamie moved over and inspected Sophie's hand. 'Do you think he is a nice man?'

Jane nodded. 'I think maybe he is.'

CHAPTER SIXTEEN

After the evening meal, Mac returned to collect the dishes and Mark was with him. Jamie ran to his dad and they hugged long and hard. Jane picked Sophie up and walked over to him. She saw the hurt on his face as he saw Sophie's bandaged hand.

He kissed Sophie on her head. 'I'm so sorry,' he whispered as Sophie held up her poorly hand to him.

'You have to make the crystal. I shouldn't have asked you not to,' Jane said urgently.

Mark put his arm around her. 'It was my decision and not yours.' He glanced round to see where Mac was, but no one was in the room with them.

Jane looked at him, puzzled.

He drew his head close to her ear as if kissing her cheek. 'Mac's going to find Stan,' he whispered, 'but he can't go until lunchtime tomorrow.'

Jane stiffened. 'But…' she began.

Mark kissed her on the lips, silencing her words.

When they parted, he returned to her ear. 'Don't worry, the crystal is made.'

Jane could hardly hear him; he was speaking so softly.

He continued quickly, 'Be careful what you say.'

He pulled away and touched her face. 'Everything will be okay,' he reaffirmed in his normal tone of voice. 'Ferrand will have the crystal by lunchtime. I don't want you or the children hurt again.'

Jane nodded.

He dropped to his knees and put his hands on Jamie's shoulders. 'I need you to be brave, Jamie. You need to help Jane with Sophie. Can you do that?'

Jamie nodded and stood a little straighter. Mark drew the boy into him and kissed the top of his head. As he stood up, he ruffled Jamie's hair.

Mark smiled at Sophie and tickled her tummy. 'You'll be going home soon.'

Sophie smiled back at him.

He offered his arms out and gently took her from Jane. He held her close, his eyes fixed on her bandaged hand. After a few minutes Sophie struggled to be put down, so he kissed her head and lowered her to the floor.

Mac reappeared at the door and indicated their time was up.

'I have to go,' he said to the children and hugged and kissed them both. When he came to Jane, he pulled her into his arms and kissed her with an urgent passion.

Jane gripped him tight and yielded to the force of his kiss.

He pulled back and gently touched her face. 'I love you so much. Thank you for being here with me.' He looked down at the children. 'And for being here for them too.'

Mac grunted urgently from the door. 'It's time!'

Mark returned to Mac, but stopped as he was about to go through the door. He looked back and gave Jane and the children a weak smile before Mac ushered him out of the room.

Alarm bells were ringing in Jane's head. Mark was acting like he was saying goodbye. What was he going to do? What could he do? She grasped her fingers together over her stomach. That empty feeling was back again and reinforcing itself, causing an uneasiness to creep through her body. Was this the end? She didn't want to believe that, she couldn't believe that. Her hope was with Mac finding Stan, because without Stan's help she knew they were not getting away from Ferrand alive.

Sophie tugged at her trouser leg, bringing Jane back from her thoughts. She picked her up and walked over to the bed. Jamie followed behind. 'Time for a story before bed, I think.' She looked at their eager faces and picked up a book about dreams.

★ ★ ★

Jane was sitting on her bed listening to the children sleep when the door opened and the spotty man who had picked her up from the motel with Mac came in.

He grinned at her. 'Boss wants to see yer.'

Jane's stomach sank and her legs seized up as she tried to get off the bed. All her body wanted to do was resist any movement towards the door and she had to fold her arms across her stomach to stop herself from heaving up all over the floor.

'Where's Mac?' she said, hoping against hope he could stop this from happening.

The man just shrugged.

Jane followed him to the main room. Her eyes viewed each door and window they passed, in an imagined attempt to find an escape from what was about to happen. They reached the room and he opened the door. As she moved past him, he leaned in and she could smell tobacco and alcohol on his breath.

'When the Boss is finished, it's you and me, baby.'

The door closed behind her.

The room was dimly lit, but she could see Ferrand by the table. A chair was ominously placed in the centre of the room and a side table with a closed box on it was close by.

'Come in and sit down,' Ferrand ordered coldly.

Jane forced herself to walk towards the chair.

'No. Here at the table.'

Jane faltered for a moment, surprised.

She moved past the chair and sat on the seat Ferrand now held out for her. Cautiously, she watched him pour some water into a glass and place it in front of her.

He sat in the chair next to her. 'I want you to tell me about your vision of Atlantis,' he said softly.

Jane opened her mouth and closed it again. How did he know about that?

Mark's whispers came to mind and she realised the laboratory, and most likely the children's room, must have listening devices in them. She cleared her throat. 'I don't know what you want me to say.'

Ferrand leapt at her, his fingers grasping her hair, yanking her head back sharply.

Jane yelped in pain.

"I said tell me what you saw.'

She saw spittle on his lips before he flung her head forward onto the table.

Jane held back her cry and closed her eyes against the pain.

Ferrand retook his seat as Jane sat up and composed herself. She told him sparingly what she saw.

He flew at her again, his fist finding her cheekbone where he had slapped her earlier.

Jane ricocheted back against the chair.

He grabbed her by the throat and half-lifted her off the seat.

She could hardly breathe and clawed at his hands until he let her go. She fell back onto the chair, gasping.

Ferrand drew closer. 'Tell me about the power crystal.'

Jane looked at him; his eyes were wild and his face stiff with anger. 'I don't know,' she croaked.

Jane saw a flash of uncontrollable rage flicker across his face before his fists began to hammer into her body.

She didn't know how long the onslaught lasted, but she lost consciousness and was just coming to when she felt a pair of hands lift her from the floor. She couldn't see too clearly out of one eye as it had swollen up, forcing the eyelids to merge together, but she could hear Ferrand in the background. He was ranting and screaming obscenities somewhere in the room.

'Easy now,' Mac's deep, soft tone whispered as he drew her into his body and carried her back to her room. Once inside, he laid her on her bed and brought cool rags to bathe her face.

His touch was gentle, but hurt like mad. It was as if all her nerves were exposed. Even the few tears she wept, stung.

'Keep this against your eye and it will go down,' he said.

Jane nodded very carefully. Her body was only now registering the aches and pains from the multiple growing bruises from Ferrand's attack. There didn't seem to be any place above her waist that didn't hurt.

Mac got up. 'Try to rest,' he said before moving to the door.

Jane watched him through her good eye and as he went to exit, he encountered the spotty guy.

'Boss says I can have her,' he said, trying to squeeze past Mac's bulky frame.

Mac took him by the throat and forced him against the wall. 'You go anywhere near her and you won't be breathing for much longer.'

Jane saw the man's frantic head nod before Mac threw him out of the room.

She closed her good eye and after a few minutes she was asleep.

★ ★ ★

It was a presence in the room that woke her and before she could react, a hand came across her mouth, pushing her head back into the pillow. She widened her good eye, trying to see who her attacker was and in the next second a light from a small torch appeared between them. It was Mac.

He put a finger to his lips and removed his hand when she nodded. He showed her two pieces of cloth and brought a small bottle out from his coat pocket. He sprinkled a few drops of the liquid onto each of the cloths and put the bottle away.

Jane quietly eased herself up, looking at him curiously.

He pointed to the children and handed Jane one of the cloths.

She realised he wanted to chloroform the children. He was helping them escape.

In the torchlight, she silently moved over to where Sophie lay and gently placed the cloth over her nose and mouth, holding it for only a few moments. She saw Mac do the same with Jamie. Sophie didn't wake, but Jamie momentarily opened his eyes before closing them again.

She lifted Sophie from the bed and followed Mac, who was carrying Jamie, to the bathroom. She hesitated at the door, doubting what was happening, until in the dim light of the torch, she saw Stan framed in the bathroom's bar-less window. All her worries disappeared and she had to stop herself from crying out with joy at seeing him.

Stan took Jamie from Mac and stood aside while Mac switched off the torch and climbed outside. Stan passed the boy through the window and Mac disappeared for a moment before returning empty-handed.

Stan motioned Jane to come forward and gently took Sophie from her. He put the child into Mac's waiting arms and Mac moved away from the window.

Jane eased herself through the window and jumped the short distance to the ground. Stan was right behind her.

Outside it was very dark with no moon or starlight penetrating the heavily clouded night sky. Jane took a moment to adjust her eyes and could just make out another man standing by Mac a few feet away. He was holding Jamie.

Stan caught hold of her arm and quickly led her away from the house to a place in the fence where they had got in. Once through the fence, they made their way silently over rough terrain and round the side of a mountain until the house was out of sight. A few yards further on, hidden amongst the bushes, was a car.

Mac opened the back door and protected Jamie's head as the other man eased himself in before slipping in himself with Sophie.

Stan escorted Jane to the passenger front side and opened the door for her. 'Missed me?' he said.

'You don't know how much,' she whispered, relief bringing tears to her eyes.

He squeezed her arm gently. 'You're okay now.'

Jane nodded and slipped into the car.

Stan got into the driver's side and moments later they were speeding away. It was then that Jane realised they had left Mark behind.

They drove for what seemed a long time, but in reality was no longer than half an hour. Jane didn't speak; she was trying to cope with the feelings she was experiencing at leaving Mark at that place. She was worried about him and what was going to happen once Ferrand found out they were gone. Then there was the guilt because she was so relieved to be free and away from there. In fact, the relief overwhelmed everything else. She felt so safe in Stan's care that she didn't want to go back ever and this made her guilt even worse for it felt like she was abandoning Mark to his fate.

Stan pulled off the road and down a dirt track to a small holding set back a mile from the road. The house was long and on two levels, with a porch to the front door and a veranda above it. Fenced areas on each side of the house contained horses and a hay shed stood at the rear. Stan pulled the car into the hay shed and cut the engine. A light came on from outside the car and Jane could see another man dressed in combat gear sat on a haystack, a rifle laid over his knees.

Stan got out. 'Okay, Jack?' he said, as he made his way round to Jane's door.

The man just nodded.

Stan opened the passenger door and smiled at Jane as he offered her his hand.

She took hold of it and eased herself from the car.

His smile dropped away suddenly when he saw her in the light. 'What the f…'

Jane felt a rush of heat surge all the way to her head. Her vision blurred and the last thing she heard was Stan saying, 'Are you all right?'

When she opened her eyes again she was laid on a bed and Stan was gently placing cool cloths on her forehead.

He noticed she was awake and smiled. 'You look like crap.'

Jane quickly reached forward and hugged him. 'Thank you, thank you so much,' she whispered into his shoulder and neck.

Stan didn't say anything until she drew back from him. 'You need to thank Mac as well.'

Jane looked at him, puzzled.

'We wouldn't have got to you without his help,' Stan continued.

'So he found you?'

Stan shook his head. 'I used a tracking implant in Mark to locate you.'

Jane was still trying to understand.

'I put an implant in Mark's shoulder at the motel before we left for the meeting in Sedona.'

She remembered the slap and Mark wincing. She nodded.

Stan touched her bruised face. 'Sorry it took so long to get to you, but I needed some help.'

Jane realised he was referring to the men he was with.

'They're ex-army buddies.'

'But where does Mac come into it?'

Stan's smile broadened. 'Mac's an old friend. When I saw him bring you to the meeting, I was surprised, but I knew I could trust him to help me if necessary and I knew he wouldn't try to stop me either.' He got up and helped her to her feet. 'I spotted Mac leaving the house this evening and intercepted him at the fence gate. Once I made contact with him, it was easy to get round the guards and get you and the children.'

'But what about Mark? Ferrand's going to be furious.'

He put his arm around her and gave her a gentle squeeze. 'He'll be fine. I've spoken to him. It was important to him I got you and the children to safety first.'

'When are you going back?'

Stan looked away.

'Stan, when…'

He moved to the door. 'Soon.'

Jane caught hold of his arm. 'How soon?'

Stan faced her and he looked serious. 'I need to plan it, Jane. Ferrand will be on guard now and it won't be easy.'

He must have seen the panic in her eyes for he quickly added, 'Mark won't come to any harm. He's too valuable. And without you or the children as leverage, Ferrand won't be able to make him complete the work.' He touched her face and drew her to him, gently kissing her forehead. 'Don't worry, okay?'

Jane nodded and her shoulders relaxed. She knew he was right, but something was niggling at the back of her mind.

'Come on, I'll show you where the children are and then we'll have a coffee with Mac.'

CHAPTER SEVENTEEN

It was late when Jane went to bed and she snuggled into the pillow. Her body was hurting and every movement seemed to highlight another bruise or painful area. Also, there was something else: a feeling she had experienced before, causing her insides to be like a deep, dark cavern, waiting and expecting something to fall into it. It was a warning to her that something was wrong. She drew a deep breath; what could this be? Was it to do with Mark?

After a few deep breaths she thought about the meadow and her guides and was instantly there. Spirit Wind was waiting for her at the edge of the forest. She rushed over to him, feeling desperate and afraid. 'Something is wrong and I don't know what it is or what to do,' she sputtered.

Spirit Wind raised his hands to calm her.

'You must tell me what I must do!'

Spirit Wind said nothing; he just watched her with gentle eyes and a calm expression.

Jane swallowed a gulp of air and then took a slow, deep breath. She felt the tension melt from her, slipping off her shoulders like a blanket of snow sliding off a roof. She gave a big sigh and saw Spirit Wind nod. 'I'm sorry,' she said.

He turned and walked into the wood and Jane followed him to the campfire in the clearing where they had been before.

He lit the fire and sat down, indicating that Jane should sit next to him. He held out his hand. 'I can only show you what has happened before,' he said quietly.

'I've seen it. I know what happens. It isn't going to help!' Jane hugged herself in annoyance.

Spirit Wind continued to offer her his hand. 'What you will see is from a time before Atlantis. A time when Great Spirit created all that is. You will see the first disaster man created.'

Jane relaxed her arms and looked at him. 'You seem a little concerned.'

He nodded. 'To see this has much consequence. It will ignite raw emotions in you.'

'Will it give me my answer?'

'I believe so.'

Jane straightened her back and gave him her hand…

★ ★ ★

Immediately, she was transported to a beautiful land, tropical in temperature, with vast plains. There were no mountains, but the low tree-filled hills were full of luxuriant tropical plants with the valleys covered in grazing grasses and tilled fields. Slow-running streams and rivers intersected the land, forming curves and bends around the forested hills, bringing water to the rich fertile ground. Everywhere she looked there were bright, sweet-smelling flowers and palm trees. In places, where the land was wide and low, the rivers formed large lakes surrounded by an array of lotus and other colourful flowers, with butterflies and hummingbirds darting from blossom to blossom.

Jane marvelled at the beauty of colour around her, the sweet songs of the birds in the trees and bushes, the fragrant scents lingering in the warm air and the feeling of complete wellness coming from everything. It made her feel wonderful.

She noticed broad, smooth roads crossing the land like a spider's web, the paving stones so connected that they looked seamless. At intervals along the roads were white temples and palaces of stone and at the centre of the spider's web was an open-topped pyramid.

Where the rivers met the ocean there were ports. Some ships were trading goods while others looked like passenger or entertainment ships, containing many people from different lands who were laughing and enjoying themselves.

She moved through the city encountering many fair-skinned, blond-haired people dressed in robes of colourful fine cotton or silk. They were busy collecting plants from the natural fields surrounding the houses.

At a junction of two roads she stopped and watched a young woman approach, and touch a tree. Its branches quivered as if replying to her silent communication and she took several of its leaves. Jane got the impression that everyone here was connected to and in harmony with nature and each other. Even the sun was pleasantly warm and the wind gentle and caressing. Nothing seemed harsh or cold. This felt like paradise.

She made her way to the centre of the city and the pyramid. It looked similar to the one in Atlantis, with its jewelled walls and open top, but this one had a smaller room at its front where all doors and windows were open to the elements. She went inside.

The room was crowded with women cradling babies and toddlers in their arms. They smiled as she moved through them. In the centre of the room under the open roof was a large circular pool with a beautiful, pale pink crystal in the centre. Its colour was reflected in the water, giving everything a warm, pink glow.

Jane could feel the crystal's vibration immediately in her heart and she felt overwhelmed with love and compassion.

Standing in the pool, with just a brief slip covering her body, was a young blonde-haired woman. Her skin was a golden colour and her eyes seemed to melt into dishes of softness. She was gently bathing a baby in the water while the mother waited at the edge. When she had finished, she beckoned the mother into the water and put the baby in her arms. The mother and child lay quietly, allowing the pink, soft water to flow over their bodies.

Jane felt the emotional bliss flowing into them and herself, even though she was at the pool edge. It was hard to move away, but she carried on through the room and into the pyramid. She recognised the crystal and tripod immediately and the man attending it looked like Mark, although his hair was long and pulled back off his face.

When he saw her, he smiled and stopped what he was doing. 'Solaras, it is a good day made even better with your return.'

Jane grinned, feeling a rising excitement in her body as she rushed over to him.

Mark took her into his arms, his eyes alive and bright as he gently touched his lips to hers. He kissed her long and hard, pushing his body into her, his need expressed in the pressure of his lips on her mouth and the touch of his hands on her skin. He finally pulled back from his kiss. 'I have so missed you.'

Jane's heart was beating with a passion she could hardly control. The sensual pleasure of his touch, his taste and his smell excited her so much that she wanted to make love to him that very instant.

She thought her heart would burst in her chest, she felt so

happy. Mark was part of her soul; he made her feel whole and complete. 'I love you.'

Mark smiled back. 'You are my life and will be for eternity.'

A young woman entered the chamber, saw them and quickly excused herself.

Jane eased herself from his arms and said, 'So what have you been busy doing during my absence?'

'I have perfected a crystal so its energy will stabilise our motherland.'

'How?'

He frowned and then chuckled. 'You are always joking with me. You gave us the idea and for that we will always be grateful.'

Jane hid her surprise and quickly said, 'Show me.'

She walked around the tripod, staring at the crystal. 'How is it different?'

Mark excitedly pointed to the crystal's faces. 'I have adjusted the angles of its face. It will amplify the energy it gives out.'

Jane closed her eyes. This was exactly how it was in Atlantis, but how could she stop it here?

A soft voice behind her interrupted them. 'My beautiful daughter, you have returned.'

Jane turned to see a tall, thin, elderly man with an elongated head, who despite the grey beard and hair seemed to walk with the ease and grace of someone much younger. He hugged her.

'What news of the teachings?'

Jane didn't know how to respond.

'Are our Naacals spreading the word?'

Jane nodded.

'That is wonderful. Soon everyone will be able to

experience the love and wonder of the creator and all will be well.' He kissed her on the forehead and left.

Jane turned back to Mark. 'I'm worried about what you have created here.'

Mark looked surprised. 'Why? It will bring balanced energy to our land.'

'I think it will be too powerful. It could destabilise the forces beneath us.'

Mark looked at her, worried; he pondered a moment. 'I will look into that for you, but I feel, that as it is, there will be no problem.'

'I hope so. Now I must spend some time at home. I'll see you later?'

Mark smiled and his face beamed. 'Yes.'

As Jane moved to leave, he grasped her hand. 'You are staying, aren't you? I couldn't bear to be away from you again.'

'I am not intending to go anywhere. We'll have lots of time to be together.'

Jane made her way to the open archway to the street and as she got there, a man entered and walked past her, nodding his head. His looks resembled Ferrand in every way, although the man was younger. She stopped and watched him disappear inside. Should she go after him, and if she did, what could she do or say? She decided not to and walked out into the street.

Further along the road there was a large palace that seemed familiar to her. It felt like this could be her home and she entered it, unconsciously knowing exactly where to go.

When she reached the large reception room, with its lush carpets and rich drapes, her vision blurred and when it cleared she was standing at a long wooden table in the centre with her father. It was dark and she assumed she had moved to a different time.

Her father looked worried.

"What is it?"

The sudden earth tremor caught her by surprise and she grabbed the table to steady herself. She looked around frantically as a deep rumble shook the air.

'Solaras,' her father called and beckoned her to him.

'What is happening?'

He shook his head sadly. 'I have failed you all.'

'Why?'

'I should have listened to your warning years ago. You were right; the motherland will die.'

'Tell me, Father, what is happening?'

He pulled her to him and hugged her. When she eased away, she saw he was crying. 'I should have stopped Fergus, but what he said made sense.'

'What, Father, what?'

'Marajai's crystal worked at first. It brought our motherland's energy up to a new level. It gave us a stable climate and bountiful crops.'

The floor shook again and the rumble that followed deepened. He gripped her tighter. 'The elders said he had the ability to tap into our creator's energy and it would bring more wonders to us, but the energy needed balancing.' He shook his head. 'I couldn't let them use you, that's why I sent you to our colonies again, with the Naacals.'

Jane suddenly realised that Marajai was Mark and that she had to find the elders to learn what they needed her to do. She pulled away from her father. 'It's okay. We can fix this.'

Her father shook his head, but Jane didn't wait for his reply. She ran into the street. Buildings were shaking and people were running into the temples and palaces, looking for comfort and protection. One of the temples seemed to stand out above the rest and she headed for it. Inside was an altar, the same as the one she saw in Atlantis, where she had met Lamar. Around the altar were two elderly men and two women. One woman was older than the other; all of them were extremely tall and had elongated heads. They were holding hands and streaming their energy into a crystal ball hanging above an amulet.

She rushed up to them. 'What can I do? What can I do?'

They stopped and stared at her. The youngest woman, whose beautiful face was shrouded in worry, answered her in a deep, rich voice. 'You are too late. You should have been with him.'

'I don't understand.'

'Only the divine feminine can bring balance to the energy download and you weren't there.'

Another shake of the floor nearly toppled Jane from her feet. 'But I must be able to do something.'

The elders all shook their heads and the woman spoke again. 'Fergus has tainted the boy and if he gets to use the crystal for the power he seeks, there will be worldwide destruction, pain and fear.'

'But there must be something we can do?' Jane yelled above the crashing sound of what sounded like thunder.

The elders turned their attention back to the crystal ball. They magnified their input of energy until the crystal ball began to shine and emit a high-pitched hum. A beam of light erupted from it, shooting across the room and piercing the engraved marble pillar by the door, splitting it apart. In the dust from the explosion an image began to take shape.

Jane looked at the young woman, confused.

'I am sorry, Solaras, but we have to ensure the power Fergus desires does not leave here.'

'What have you done?'

'We have summoned one of the sacred four. The Great Primary Force that will end our existence.'

Jane looked at the swirling mass of energy and saw the figure of a man take form. He was dressed like a guardian from Atlantis, with a hooded cloak and a staff in his hand, which had a magnificent white crystal on the top. He moved away and out of the temple.

Jane rushed off after him. She followed him through the streets, heading towards the pyramid. His pace was swift and true while she struggled to keep her footing with every shake and wobble the land produced. He soon left her behind.

Eventually, she reached the pyramid and rushed through the crumbling archway. She saw the tripod and crystal in the centre of the room. Mark was kneeling beside it with his hands touching the crystal. He was shaking uncontrollably in a shaft of bright light coming down from the sky. It was engulfing him and flowing into the crystal through his hands.

The crystal was taking in the energy in a pulsating regular pattern, but the vibrational energy coming from it was fluctuating in all directions. Some of the energy hit her and she fell to the floor, her strength suddenly depleted.

'Marajai!' she screamed.

He glanced over to her and she saw fear on his face.

'I can't stop it. I'm so sorry.'

Jane tried to get up, but her body wouldn't move. She twisted her head and saw Fergus, Ferrand's former self, just off to one side of the crystal. He was holding a small three-pointed crystal in the shape of a pyramid to his chest and it looked like he was drawing energy from the large crystal into himself.

'More, more,' he yelled, his face alight with power.

Something moved just off to the right of the crystal and Jane saw the Great Primary Force. He raised his staff and directed the crystal end towards Mark.

'No…no. I'm here, I can save us,' Jane screamed, but it was too late.

A beam of intense blue light pierced the bubble of energy around Mark and entered his chest. The force of its impact sent Mark backwards across the room and the energy beam from above immediately dissipated.

The Primary Force turned to her and Jane recognised its face; it was Stan. His free hand moved out towards her and she felt herself being lifted off the floor by something invisible and carried back to the pyramid entrance. As she was moving away, her attention was drawn to Fergus.

He looked pale and a little confused. He was staring in shock at the crystal he was holding, then he looked up and focused on the Primary Force. His face darkened with rage and with a yell of fury he charged.

Jane abruptly hit the floor.

The Primary Force turned to fend him off, his staff slamming down onto Fergus' head, the crystal tip slicing open a cavernous gash in his skull.

The hit didn't kill him and he staggered past Jane holding his head, blood dripping through his fingers.

Jane searched the room for Mark. He was lying with his back to her not too far from the crystal. She forced herself to her feet and rushed over to him. The air around her felt heavy and thick.

'Mark, Mark.' She eased him onto his back. There was

a gaping hole in his chest where his heart had been and his wide, staring eyes told her he was dead. She burst into tears and rested her head on his shoulder; her desire to carry on living had flat-lined, her heart blown away too. An emptiness was filling her whole being with a cold numbness she would never be able to warm again.

She lay with Mark and in the blur of her tears she watched the Primary Force move over to the crystal. He stepped into the place where Mark had been and lifted his staff high before bringing it down sharply so the crystal tip smashed onto the pulsating point of the tripod's crystal. The whole room became as bright as the sun and a beam of pure light came down through the crystal and tripod, into the earth.

The floor shook violently, sending jolts through Jane's body as if she was a bouncing ball. She continued to watch the Primary Force as he became engulfed in the light and just as his body began to disappear she saw his hand stretch out to her.

Her body began to rise and she desperately grabbed for Mark as she floated across the floor away from him. The force upon her was too strong and she was carried out through the archway where it suddenly disappeared and she fell, tumbling down the steps to the ground outside the collapsing pyramid.

In the street a group of men and women stopped and helped her up. They guided her to a boat tethered on the river's edge.

Jane hardly noticed what was happening. Her body was moving without any conscious effort from her as her mind was numb and refused to function. Someone helped her to a seat at the rear and when everyone was on, the boat skimmed over the water like it wasn't touching it at all. It continued along the river at speed until it finally came out into the main estuary where the water around them was bubbling and churning as if they were in a boiling cauldron.

Jane stared at the scene from the back of the boat. The land each side of the river was heaving up violently, exploding in plumes of volcanic activity. Streams of black smoke were spiralling up into the air, trying to darken the sky. From the flames leaping from the lava-filled gaping holes in the land, red hot boulders were shooting out, travelling like fiery comets, colliding and crashing through any buildings that still remained standing.

The sun was setting, yet the sky remained bright in the flames of the eruptions. The lower the sun got, the deeper the red and it began to look like a river of blood flowing through the dark, black, dust clouds.

Jane couldn't stop watching even as the boat picked up speed and sped away. She kept her sight on the place where her home had been even when they reached shore. It was dark now, yet she could still see the deep red and yellow glow hovering over where the motherland was. More flashes of flames erupted from the horizon, reaching high in the sky like streaks of lightning coming from the earth herself. At the same time, the water at her feet began to recede from the beach, just like the prelude to a tsunami, and as it did, the screams of thousands of people echoed over the water.

The people from the boat fell to their knees crying and weeping, their hands covering their ears, blocking out the suffering of their brothers and sisters.

Jane could feel their emotions vibrate through her body and she dropped to her knees, praying for it to stop. A moment later there came a thunderous sound of rushing water cascading over a giant waterfall. It drowned out the death cries of all those who had been left behind and the deep, rich glow on the horizon finally went out, leaving darkness and silence to take over.

Jane gasped herself back from her meditation and felt Spirit Wind's hand squeeze hers. Her body shuddered and convulsed as deep-rooted sobs surfaced. Her eyes couldn't contain the constant flow of tears as they rushed over onto her cheeks like a river bursting its banks.

She rolled over to lie on the floor. Her cries and sobs shaking her body, refusing to stop; her mind desperately trying to blank out and forget what she had seen. 'I… I… can't stop c… crying.'

'Your body remembers,' Spirit Wind said softly.

The deep emptiness in her was like nothing she had felt before. Her cries were coming from a place beyond her body, a place of deep memory attached to her soul.

'This is the first hurt you ever experienced. One you hid from yourself in all of your lives.'

'I… I can see why…' Jane could hardly speak for her tears just kept on coming.

Spirit Wind just held her hand, and gradually, after several more bouts of sobs, Jane was eventually able to sit up and take a hiccup of breath. She looked at him through swollen eyes and saw he was crying too. 'All those poor people,' she managed to say.

'Sixty-four million voices.' Spirit Wind paused as if to swallow. 'My people heard them, the Mayan people heard them, the Peruvian and Indian people heard them.' He put his arm around her. 'Our motherland was destroyed in the belief it would save our sister land, Atlantis, and the spiritual teachings of our creator in our other colonies.'

'But it didn't.'

'No. The Primary Force failed. It was supposed to destroy

the people who would bring the destructive force down. One escaped, so it did the next best thing it could. It destroyed the land that created it.'

'Ferrand escaped?'

'Yes.'

'But what about Atlantis?'

Spirit Wind eased her away. 'It failed there too, in two ways.'

'What ways?'

'It didn't save you, and Ferrand escaped again.'

Jane remembered the hesitation the guardian showed before disappearing with the tripod. She leaned forward and poked the fire with a stick, her mind going over all the information. 'The elders said only the divine feminine can bring balance to the energy download.'

Spirit Wind nodded. 'The motherland was destroyed because the masculine was not balanced and man's ego was allowed to commandeer the need for the power as the way forward.'

'I was the divine feminine, but my father wouldn't give me up.'

'There is always a risk in creating such energy. His love for you made him want to protect you and he let fear cloud his judgement. He thought you would be destroyed if you did it, but in trying to save you, he brought on the destruction. He was wrong. It was a decision that left the world in turmoil and lost it the wonder of the creator's gift.'

'How do you know all this?'

Spirit Wind tried to smile. 'Because I was your father in that lifetime.'

Jane stared at him and saw the sadness in his face. She leaned over to him and kissed his cheek. 'We are all part of this, aren't we?'

He nodded. 'The land of Mu was the motherland of man, where all creation was born. It and Atlantis were destroyed and sent to the depths of the earth to be forgotten, but our souls remember.'

'I remember the love, happiness and contentment of the people. No one wanted for anything. They were peaceful and living a wonderful life in harmony with everything.'

'That was the destiny of all of us. Our creator designed it for us.'

'So what happened? Why didn't it continue with the other colonies?'

Spirit Wind pondered for a moment. 'When the motherland was destroyed, Atlantis became the guardians of the teachings, but without the love and support of the motherland's elders, the masculine side began to dominate. The new spirit teachers sent away the Naacals. They learned they could control the people by the use of fear more easily. Their egos craved the power this gave them and they created different teachings.'

'And the Naacals, what happened to them?'

'They hid themselves and the sacred tablets, offering knowledge only to those who found them.'

Jane sighed heavily; if only it hadn't happened, life would have been so beautiful and wonderful. 'So what now?' she said quickly, not wanting to dwell on what mankind had lost.

'You are the divine feminine; you have the power to stop this.'

Jane thought about it. 'If Mark brings down the energy on his own, even with the approaching star, the destruction will happen again. So, like in Africa, I need to be present for us to be safe?'

'Yes, I believe so, but if the power ends up in the hands of a corrupt man it will still bring destruction.'

Jane nodded. The last thing she wanted was for Ferrand to control it. 'So the best thing to do is to stop Mark bringing the energy down at all.'

'That would be the ideal solution.'

Jane stood up. 'Mark said he wouldn't give Ferrand the power and now the children and I are safe, Ferrand cannot force him to do it.'

Spirit Wind stood with her. 'Will he be able to keep his promise no matter what is done to him?'

'I don't know.' She recalled the beating Ferrand gave her and even though she didn't have the information he wanted, if she had, would she have endured it so long or just given in? 'It is hard to say, especially when you are in pain. I don't know what he would do.'

'Let Great Spirit guide you in your actions.'

She hugged him long and hard. 'Thank you.'

'Goodbye,' he said, sadness touching his face.

Jane looked into his soft eyes and accepted that this could be the last time they would meet. As she walked back to the meadow she thought about what she should do. *If Mark is forced to use the energy, I need to be there, but how can I do that except by going back?*

CHAPTER EIGHTEEN

Jane woke up and wiped remnants of tears from her eyes. It was still dark; her watch showed it had only been an hour since she had got into bed. The events of the meditation troubled her and her body felt exhausted, her eyes sore as if she had really shed those thousands of tears. She knew what she had to do, but the thought of going back to Ferrand's place terrified her. She didn't want to go. The man was cruel and sadistic. What would he do to her if he got hold of her again?

She shivered violently.

Why couldn't she stay here, safe and protected? That was what had happened in her past life in Mu, but it had been fatal to all those people.

She got out of bed and opened the patio doors to the small balcony outside her room.

Why couldn't she stay here? Stan was going back for Mark. She didn't have to put herself in danger again. But what about Ferrand? Stan could kill him when he rescued Mark; do the thing he had failed to do in the past.

She shuddered. *What am I doing thinking like this? I'm now planning someone's death. There has to be another way; please, there has to be.*

Silently, she slipped out and onto the floor, resting her back against the wall. It was pleasantly warm from the day's sun and the evening sky was cloudless, exposing a multitude of sparkling stars. As she looked up, a shooting star sped across the sky and she made a wish. The only wish she could make.

A shuffling of feet on gravel drew her attention to the path beside the porch below her. A cigarette lighter clicked and she heard the intake of breath. A second gravel sound came.

'Want a drag?' The masculine voice was gruff.

She heard a second intake of breath, followed by a slow release.

'Is Stan going back to finish them off?' the gruff voice asked.

Jane's attention heightened.

'Yeah, that's what he said he was going to do. He's leaving in fifteen minutes.'

There was a brief silence and Jane held her breath, straining to hear more.

'What about the woman's bloke?'

'Nothing said about a rescue. Stan just wanted the car filled with explosives. I reckon he's going to blow the whole lot up.'

There was another intake of breath and a slow release. 'We're to babysit. He don't want any help.'

'Yeah, that's Stan for you.'

The two men moved off together and Jane waited until the sound of their footsteps was distant before she leapt to her feet and rushed back into the bedroom.

Her mind was in turmoil. Stan was going back to kill them all, including Mark. She had known something was wrong when he was vague about going back to get him. He had been hiding something from her and this was it.

What should she do?

She snatched at her trousers and blouse, swiftly dressing

while her mind continued to think. Perhaps she could confront Stan now, but if he meant to kill Mark, he'd do it anyway; she was no match to stop him. Why, why would he kill him after all they had been through?

She struggled with the buttons of her blouse, her mind still looking for answers. Of course, Stan was the Primary Force. He was going back to fulfil what he had been created for. He hadn't succeeded in the past in the motherland and in Atlantis and now this was his chance.

She slipped on her shoes. So how could she stop him? She could disable the car, but she didn't know how and he'd have another vehicle somewhere else.

Jane grasped the bedroom door handle, panic rising with each minute she hesitated. Her mind was blank; no solutions seemed to present themselves. Then a faint idea crept in, a mad idea, but one that just might work.

She opened the bedroom door just enough to see out. The corridor was empty and she slipped out and moved to the stairs. No one was about, so she went down slowly. At the bottom she paused; the kitchen was to her right, opposite the front door.

There were muffled sounds of talking and she guessed it was Stan's men. Then she heard Stan's voice come clearly over the others. 'You know the plan? I'll be back in a couple of hours. Don't tell Jane until it's over.'

She pressed her lips tightly together, suppressing the anger that wanted to make her rush in and confront him. Instead, she silently moved to the front door and slipped out.

The porch light was dim, but it showed her the steps to the gravel path. Once down them, she stepped on the grass edge and made her way round to the barn where the car was parked outside.

She lifted the boot and slipped in, wriggling her body over some hard metal shapes covered in a blanket. She eased the boot down enough so she could just see outside. Something was sticking hard into her back. She felt its shape and pulled it away. It was a rifle. She laid it across her front just as Stan emerged from the house and walked towards the car. She held her breath, hoping he wouldn't notice the boot.

He didn't. He went straight to the driver's side, got in and started the car.

Jane closed the boot onto its catch and lay back, tightly holding on to the rifle as the car moved away.

The journey was rough and she felt every bump through her bruised body. She listened intently, waiting for the sound of the car slowing to a stop. She needed to do this quickly. Surprising Stan wasn't going to be easy if she could do it at all.

The car seemed to travel a long time and the rhythmic motion dulled her attention and it was the sudden jolt of the car stopping that shook her from her daze. She gripped tightly to the barrel of the rifle. She'd only have one chance, a fraction of a second to do this.

The driver's door opened and quietly shut. She could hardly hear Stan's steps as he moved round to the back of the car. The boot lifted and Stan leaned in.

The interior light spotlighted Jane and she saw the look of surprise on his face a fraction of a second before the butt of the rifle hit his head. He fell backwards and to the floor. Jane was up and out of the boot quicker than she believed possible. She stood slightly away and watched as Stan, dazed and disoriented, tried to get up. 'J… Jane?'

'You bastard. I won't let you kill him.' Jane hit him again.

Stan collapsed to the floor and didn't move.

Jane looked at him and began to shake. She hadn't

meant to hit him so hard, but she needed to stop him. She nudged him with the rifle barrel; he didn't move. Was he pretending? Waiting for her to get close, so he could grab her? Jane took the chance and touched his neck with her fingers, feeling the artery for a pulse. It was there. A small gash on his forehead was bleeding across his face, but clear of his airway.

Jane dropped the rifle and looked around. She recognised the area as the place where Stan had parked before, when he had rescued her and the children. She got her bearings and found a small pathway, which she hoped would lead her back to Ferrand's place. She shivered, she didn't know what she was going to do when she got there; perhaps she could find a way to get Mark out. All she was sure of was this incessant need in her to get to him.

Jane followed the path, her eyes adjusting to the darkness. It seemed different somehow, but maybe it was because she hadn't taken much notice of it before. The path ended up on a road and Jane was sure she hadn't walked on a road last time. As she pondered which way to go, she saw a car approaching. It looked like Stan's car and she knew there was nowhere she could hide or run. Perhaps she could talk to him, persuade him not to kill Mark; that would be if he listened after the battering she had given him.

The car pulled up alongside her and the window slid down. She bent down about to apologise when she smelled cigarettes and booze. She quickly straightened, but not quickly enough as a hand shot out and grabbed her blouse.

'Hello, baby, I missed you.'

Jane yanked backwards into the grip of another man who she hadn't seen get out of the car. The car door opened and the sleazy, spotty man moved in close. She felt his hands grab her breasts and squeeze them hard. Jane stared back at him, ignoring the pain.

'I'm going to be Ferrand's number one boy when I bring you in,' he smirked before trying to kiss her mouth. Jane turned her head away from him.

He laughed. 'But first I'm going to get what I'm owed.' He tore her blouse apart, exposing her bra and slobbered into her cleavage.

Jane tried to draw her body away.

A mobile phone rang and she heard the spotty man moan. He continued to push his hands under her bra. The phone's tone grew louder as if urgent.

'It's the Boss. You better answer it,' said the man holding her.

The spotty man growled and moved away. He pulled the phone from his pocket. 'YES!'

The sound that came back was harsh and unrelenting.

'Yes. No. Sorry, sir. Yes, immediately.' He put the phone away. 'We have to get back now,' he told the other man. His face came close to Jane's. 'Next time, baby, nothing's going to stop me.' He got back into the car and Jane was forced into the back with the other man.

She pulled her blouse across her body and sat still. She was going back to Mark, but not in the way she had hoped. This could go badly.

★ ★ ★

At the house, Jane got out of the car. She didn't resist or make any move to be awkward. She needed to be there. The spotty man pushed the other man out of the way and took her arm, squeezing it hard. He moved her forward and they all walked into the house to the main room where Ferrand was waiting. The look of pure joy was evident on Ferrand's face when he saw her.

'Found her on the road, Boss. No sign of the children.'

Jane knew he hadn't even looked for them.

'You've earned yourself a bonus, Billy,' Ferrand said, as he moved over to her. He touched her hair. 'You're going to get me what I want,' he said smoothly. 'Billy, go get Adrian, it's time.'

Billy left the room and Ferrand turned to the other man standing by Jane. 'In the alcove with her and no noise.'

The big man walked her to the alcove, pulling her back into the shadows to a place dark enough not to be seen by those in the room.

A moment later Mark entered with the crystal. He seemed calm and confident as he handed it over to Ferrand.

Ferrand's face radiated with pleasure; he licked his lips and stroked the crystal's surface with a soft touch. He took it over to where the tripod was stood by the window and placed it in the metal support. The crystal immediately seemed to brighten as its tip touched the centre oval of the Vesica Piscis. He stood for several minutes watching it, then he beckoned Mark forward.

Mark remained where he was until Billy shoved him hard in the back.

'Now produce the energy,' Ferrand said, almost in a whisper.

'NO.'

Ferrand turned to him. 'You test my patience. Bring down the energy.'

'No.'

'Have you forgotten what I did to your child?'

Mark shook his head and then smiled. 'Jane and the children are safe. You can't harm them any more.'

Jane tensed and thought, *What have I done?*

Ferrand laughed a hearty laugh and Jane could see Mark's confidence waver.

'Bring her out!' Ferrand yelled.

Mark turned around and Jane saw disappointment wash over his face at the sight of her.

'Now you will bring down the energy,' Ferrand repeated as he walked over to her and pulled her forward.

Mark hesitated. He looked confused.

'Don't do it, don't—'

Ferrand had Jane by the throat, cutting off her words.

She snuffled air in through her nose while the pressure of his hand prevented her from speaking again.

He pulled her round in front of him to face Mark.

Mark's face was pale and drawn, his eyes wide, but he shook his head. 'I can't.'

Jane was dragged backwards towards the crystal and tripod.

'I will kill her, right here in front of you, if you don't.'

Mark gripped his hands into fists and stiffened his body. He stared at Ferrand with a hardened look.

Jane realised he was trying to trigger the power he had used before at Solita's house. A power that would end all of this and save them both.

He suddenly looked at her as if realising it wasn't going to happen, his eyes pleading with her for an answer.

She mouthed the words 'I love you' and slowly closed her eyes and opened them again. She hoped he would recognise her sign of acceptance of his decision.

Ferrand lost patience; his hand tightened on her throat. 'You want me to kill her?' he shouted.

Mark frantically shook his head. 'No, no.' His voice quivered as he said, 'But I can't do this.'

'Then watch her die.'

Jane started to gag and she grabbed Ferrand's hand in an attempt to ease the pressure.

Ferrand began to laugh like a mad man, his fingernails cutting into her skin, sending trickles of blood down her neck.

Jane began to thrash about; she could feel her life slowly seeping away.

'NO. Stop, I'll do it,' Mark shouted.

Ferrand's hand suddenly left her throat and his arm slid across her body, pulling her into him.

Jane gasped back her breath, heaving in the air her body so desperately needed.

'Do it. Do it now!' Ferrand commanded.

Mark walked despondingly over to the crystal and tripod. He took the crystal pyramid from his pocket and placed it on the floor before kneeling over it.

Jane saw him take a deep breath and begin to chant words in the strange language he had used in Africa. Gradually, he raised his hands above his head, feeling the air with his fingers. The air began to quiver and distort like a heatwave on the horizon.

Jane could feel the stillness in the room as if they had suddenly moved into a vacuum. She knew the energy was coming and although she was nervous, she was also calm in the knowledge that her presence would bring stability to it all.

Mark moved his hands higher, cupping the energy in his palms. Sparks of light flickered into being within the invisible ball of energy he held. They merged together into a spot of brightness that began to grow and fill the area between his hands.

He brought the energy ball down to his chest, his hands moving further apart as the spark of light got bigger and bigger. Soon it was bigger than a football and he was struggling to hold it. He stood up and moved the ball of energy to the top of the crystal.

When the ball settled on the crystal point, a shaft of light burst into existence, flowing down and into the crystal. There was a low pulsing sound and the crystal's brightness increased with each pulse as the energy flowed through it and into the ground beneath the tripod.

It was beautiful and Jane couldn't take her eyes off the crystal and pulsing light. This was pure power, the power of the creator, and she was mesmerised by it. She looked at Mark, only now realising that he seemed fixed to the crystal and the energy was spreading down his hands and into his arms.

The room shook and a deep rumble from deep beneath them rippled under the floor. The marble cracked across its length and up the far wall by the door.

Jane couldn't believe this was happening again. She was here; she was the divine feminine; all should be okay.

There came a crash like thunder and the floor split wide open, sending shards of thick rock out of the earth and into the room.

Ferrand grabbed her and forced her against the wall behind them. 'Tell me how I control the power,' he said, pushing his face close to hers.

Jane shook her head. 'I don't know.'

He pulled a knife from his back pocket and stabbed her just below her left collar bone. 'You have seen it. Tell me.'

Jane yelled out with pain as he twisted the knife in a little deeper. She was desperately trying to recall what she had seen in her meditation, but her mind was confused and still focusing on why her presence hadn't brought the energy into balance. She searched for the answers, aware that with each passing minute the destruction around them was getting worse.

The floor heaved again and they fell to the ground, shielding their heads from the falling walls. Jane caught a glimpse of Mark. The energy had moved down his arms and into his body. He was morphing out of shape and she knew the energy was absorbing him.

She frantically searched her mind for answers. What had happened in Africa? The energy had been stable. She had been present but something else must have happened. But what?

The image of the mine's shack flashed in her mind and she saw Mark hand her the master crystal to hold while he disabled the camera. She knew what she had to do.

Ferrand yanked her to her feet and his grip on her tightened. 'Tell me, damn it.'

Jane looked into his face and saw fear for the first time. She recalled the scene in the Motherland of Mu where Ferrand was taking the energy into himself. 'I will give you the answer in return for you letting me and Mark go.'

Ferrand sneered at her and she knew what he was thinking. Once he got the power, he could do anything and would destroy them both. But maybe there was some hope if she could save Mark.

'Agreed. Now tell me.'

Jane hesitated. Was she making the right decision? If she didn't act now, Mark would die. She pointed to the crystal pyramid between Mark's feet. 'You had that against your chest.'

Ferrand pushed her away and lunged for the crystal. He snatched it up and placed it to his chest, before moving closer to the tripod. A beam of energy shot from the master crystal into the pyramid and into Ferrand. His eyes closed and he laughed hysterically.

Jane shot across to Mark. She placed one hand on the master crystal and the other on Mark's shoulder. The power from the crystal was overwhelming.

Her body began to shake uncontrollably. Her skin was prickling as if intense heat was scorching it and her energy field and chakras were spinning wildly. All her organs felt like they were being twisted and squeezed out of shape, causing intense pain.

She muffled a scream by gritting her teeth and focused on staying connected to the crystal and Mark.

Gradually, the pain subsided and a warm glow began to creep into her body. The pressure on her aura and chakras stabilised and she started to relax. She saw that Mark's body was returning to its normal physical shape and sighed with relief.

The master crystal and energy began pulsing in unison: a deep, soft, strong vibration which seemed to ease the earth's turmoil. The room stopped shaking and the floor settled into its upheaved state.

Mark took a long, deep breath and released his grip on the crystal. The energy beam from the sky disappeared.

Jane eased her hand away too and cautiously turned him to face her. She didn't know what to expect. Mark had almost disappeared, almost been absorbed by the energy. How had that affected him?

Mark stared at her, his face blank, his eyes glazed.

'Mark, are you all right?'

She watched his eyes focus on her and a flicker of recognition touch his face.

'Thank you,' he said softly and took her into his arms.

Jane sensed a surge of energy flow from him into her and it felt wonderful. It reminded her of that wonderful bliss she felt when she was with him in Mu. She had him back.

As they hugged, they heard Ferrand's laughter grow louder.

They turned to face him and Mark pushed Jane behind him.

Ferrand's chest was glowing around the crystal pyramid, which had fused itself into his skin and a steady stream of energy was flowing into him from the master crystal on the tripod. His face was flush red and his whole body seemed to have grown larger with the aura around his body bright and pulsing.

'I have the power of Atlantis,' he shouted in euphoria.

He suddenly spotted them and Jane saw evil in his eyes. She knew her actions had saved Mark and the world from destruction, but she had handed Ferrand the power to rule them all.

'Time for you to die,' he declared, bringing his hands together above his head and sending lightning bolts into the air.

Mark moved forward away from Jane and stopped. He straightened his body and moved his arms out from his sides. His hands were glowing and the energy from them was pulsing in time with the master crystal. He pushed his palms forward, creating a radiating shield of energy in front of him.

Jane could see that Mark and the master crystal's energies were one.

Ferrand glared at him and clapped his hands together, sending several lightning bolts towards Mark.

Mark's energy shield absorbed the lightning, making it grow stronger.

Ferrand's face registered shock at first, then fury overwhelmed him. He cupped his hands together and drew the energy into a ball. He flung it at Mark with a scream of rage.

The force of its impact on Mark's energy shield caused the air to sizzle and explode into sparks, but Mark held his ground.

Ferrand couldn't contain his fury any longer. He rushed at Mark, sending out everything he could muster. Massive bolts of lightning began to strike all over the room.

Mark remained steady. The energy shield surrounding him was blocking Ferrand's attack and preventing him from getting closer.

Time seemed to be slow as if they were all in a vacuum that had sealed them in a portal of space.

Jane stepped back, feeling the air around her become electrified. She was having trouble breathing, her lungs struggling to process the air she was taking in. She tried to hold her breath but her body forced her to gasp more air as it began to go into spasm.

She collapsed to the floor in slow motion, her eyes fixed on the huge power bubble growing between Ferrand and Mark. It was a standoff and no one was gaining ground.

Her chest began to hurt and burn as the air became less and less and as she gasped her last few breaths, she thought she saw a long silver bullet slip through the air in front of her.

The master crystal exploded in a massive blast of light. The shockwave from it lifted her off the floor and shifted her back into the room towards the door. Her vision was lost for a second, her hearing became hollow and her body numbed, but she could breathe air again. She gulped it down, filling her lungs as deeply as she could.

She could see Ferrand lying a few feet from her, a crystal shard embedded in his chest where the pyramid had been. His breathing was shallow.

She heard a cracking sound followed immediately by another and she turned her head in the direction of the noise. Billy and Ferrand's other man were laid on the floor, and walking towards her was Stan. He walked past her to stand over Ferrand.

Ferrand drew in a sharp breath. 'Who are you?'

Stan raised his gun. 'Someone you shouldn't have fucked with.' The bullet went into Ferrand's head.

It was finally done, the task that the Atlantis guardian and the Great Primary Force had been summoned to do. Jane was glad it was over, but would Stan kill Mark too?

Mark. She suddenly realised that Mark was missing. He wasn't laid by her or by the tripod or anywhere close by. She searched the room, desperately hoping he hadn't been disintegrated by the energy. A crumpled lump of material by the alcove caught her eye. Was that him?

She tried to get up, registering for the first time pain coming from her right leg. When she looked down, she saw a piece of crystal stuck in her thigh. She struggled up onto her good leg and hobbled as fast as she could to the alcove. Stan was moving up behind her and it spurred her on. When she got closer, she saw that the lump of material was the back of Mark's blackened shirt and she was dreading what she would see when she turned him over.

She fell to her knees, ignoring the shooting pain in her

thigh and pulled his body over. Blood was covering most of his shirt from the small fragments of crystal that were stuck into his chest. She watched for his breath, her heart thumping.

'Mark! Mark!'

He opened his eyes. 'That went well.'

Jane flung herself onto him, kissing his face in relief.

She heard Stan approach and when she turned to look at him she noticed he still had his gun in his hand. 'Don't kill him. Please don't kill him.'

Stan holstered his gun and crouched down. 'Sorry I'm late,' he told Mark. 'I was delayed by a certain woman.' He fingered the bloody gash on his head.

Jane stared at him, confused.

'Just glad you showed up when you did,' Mark said, sitting up and brushing the crystal pieces off his chest.

'Are you hurt bad?'

Mark shook his head, then turned his attention to Jane.

Stan looked at her leg. 'I know just the man who can remove this for you.' He stood up, reached out his hand and pulled her to her feet.

Mark got up and slipped his arm around her waist to support her. 'Only one more thing to do now, Stan.' He nodded towards the tripod.

Stan kicked all the crystal pieces together and placed a taped package on the top. He flicked the switch on the box attached to the package and then picked up the tripod. 'I know just the lava pit for this,' he said and made his way to the door.

Jane and Mark followed him through the house to the fence without coming across any of Ferrand's men. Jane suspected they were all dead.

Once outside the fence, Stan stopped and took something

from his pocket. He gave it to Mark. 'I think you deserve to do this.'

It was a black box with a red button on it. Mark pushed the button and moments later Ferrand's house exploded and was consumed by flames.

Mark gave a big sigh of relief. 'It's finished,' he said softly. 'It's finally over.'

Jane allowed herself to smile as she thought, *In more ways than you could possibly know.*

★ ★ ★

Back at Stan's place, Mac successfully removed the crystal shard and bandaged up the knife wound on her chest. Her sleep for the remaining dark hours of the morning was dreamless and peaceful.

She woke to sunlight streaming through the window and to the sound of children's laughter from outside. She got up gently, letting her poor battered body take its time easing into the day. She didn't linger long in front of the bathroom mirror. She looked a mess, yet inside she felt wonderful. After a quick wash she made her way to the kitchen and sat at the kitchen table where she could see Mark playing with his children through the kitchen window. He looked so happy.

Stan pulled out the chair beside her and sat down. He offered her a cup of coffee, which she accepted.

She turned to him. 'I didn't get to say sorry for hitting you last night.'

He smiled. 'You must be only one of a few people who have ever caught me off guard; well done.'

'Well done? I could have killed you.'

'No. You don't have it in you, as doesn't Mark.'

She looked at him inquiringly. 'Explain.'

Stan took a sip of his coffee. 'When I got to Ferrand's place and hooked up with Mac, I spoke briefly with Mark through his window. He wanted you and the children safe, but knew while he and Ferrand were alive, you couldn't be.

'But you were going to rescue him too.'

Stan shook his head. 'Ferrand would have been relentless in getting him back, so Mark decided he was going to kill himself.'

Jane stared at him. 'No.'

'I think he would have done it to keep you and the children safe.'

Jane looked at the mug she was fingering.

'But I persuaded him to let me kill Ferrand instead.'

'Why would you do that?'

He cowered while grinning at her. 'Promise me you won't hit me again.'

Jane sat back. 'Depends on what you're going to say.'

'Well, remember, on the boat from Africa, I told you about James saving my life.'

Jane nodded.

'Hmm, well, I wasn't quite truthful with you. He did save me exactly as I told you, but what I didn't tell you was that he had been the target.'

Jane's mouth opened and closed again.

'It was James' father Ferrand got the tripod from and it was Ferrand who hired me to kill James. He also sent those men to kill me.' He took a sip of coffee before continuing. 'I have been searching for Ferrand for years, but he was elusive. No one knew what he looked like and those who did didn't live long. So when you and Mark went to stay with James, I finally found someone who could connect me to Ferrand.'

Jane sat up abruptly. 'You used us?'

'Yes, I'm sorry. Mark was the key; he knew what Ferrand looked like and Ferrand wanted him badly. I missed getting Ferrand in Africa, so tagged along with you both for the next opportunity which came when Mark went to see his ex in Tuscon.'

'But how did you know Ferrand would go for Mark there?'

'I didn't. I just prepared myself for any chance he would pick Mark up. At Tuscon I needed you to be with Mark because I knew you wouldn't let him be taken if you had been sitting in the car with me.'

'Damn right I wouldn't have.' Jane felt a stirring of annoyance.

'I saw the men arrive and I hung on, waiting for them to leave with Mark and you, but when they didn't, I returned to the house. I'm really sorry for what happened to you, Jane.'

Jane remembered the flash of guilt he had displayed when she had told him it hadn't been his fault. 'I could have been killed.'

'I know. It wasn't what I wanted to happen. That is why I wanted you to stay out of it when Mark arranged to do the swap for the children. And it would have all worked out for Mark and me if Ferrand had met Mark at the car park, job done.'

'But he didn't and you anticipated that by planting a tracking device on Mark.'

'Exactly. Unfortunately, it got complicated with you being captured and his children being held as hostages. So when I spoke to Mark, I persuaded him to just delay Ferrand and I would return to kill him once you and the children were safe.'

Jane sighed. 'A good plan, until I messed it up.'

Stan grinned. 'Yes. Until you messed it up. What possessed you to do it? And why would you think I was going to kill Mark?'

'It's a long story; I'll explain it to you later.' Jane got up and moved to the kitchen window. She watched Mark pick the children up and swing them round, their yells of delight and laughter filling the air.

Stan came and stood beside her. 'You think Mark will still have the power he used last night?'

'I don't know. I think maybe he's always had it.'

He nudged her gently. 'And what about you? Are you ready to inherit a family?'

Jane smiled. 'Yes, in every way.' She turned to him. 'And what's next for you?'

He pondered for a moment. 'Apart from shooting bad guys? I think I'll ask Fiona to marry me.'

★ ★ ★

EPILOGUE

Later:

Jane entered her meditation and returned to the meadow and wood. Spirit Wind and Three Wolves were waiting for her and she ran over to them in excitement. 'I did it, I did it.'

Spirit Wind smiled at her warmly. 'And what did you learn?'

Jane thought about it for a few minutes. 'I learned that we are all connected to each other in some way and over time. That we have immortal souls and we were created to live happy lives. But we are influenced by things that have occurred in the past, and when past events are not resolved they can impact on our future and our happiness. It has given me a lot to think about and I'm glad it's sorted now.'

Spirit Wind looked at her thoughtfully. 'So are you ready to tackle your next one?'